Old Friends

#JustFriends Series - Book 2

MARIE COLE

To my husband. Thank you for working so hard to provide for our family so that I can dabble with writing.

Old Friends

Chapter 1

I wasn't necessarily looking forward to tonight - the food was going to be wonderful but Jen's birthday dinners were always so joyless. She pretended to like the gifts we gave her but she was not very good at it. She'd long since dropped her public face around me. She reserved that for newcomers, acquaintances - tonight she'd be in the presence of unknown company so I was hopeful that we could all be civil and enjoy ourselves a little bit.

Despite everything we'd been through since high school I'd somehow managed to be civil towards her. We were far from BFFs but we did exchange an occasional email every now and again, mostly about Kent..

Several years after college I met a terrific guy and we dated for a couple of years. He moved away for work and I stayed behind without him. The relationship with him proved to me that I could love someone despite the trampling my heart had taken in my youth. A year later I met Dave at one of my wedding gigs. He flirted with me shamelessly and because he was so funny, intelligent and charming, I gave in. It probably hadn't hurt that he was extremely hot.

Tonight marked two months since Dave and I started dating and this was the first time I decided to let him meet any of my friends. If he could survive Jen and Kent, then he could survive anyone.

I inhaled deeply and expelled my breath slowly, letting the tension and anxiety leave me before I stepped out of the cab to greet my uber-handsome date, Dave. I tugged on the bottom of my hot pink hem, pulling it closer to my knees. I flashed Dave a reassuring smile as I took the arm he held out to me. He looked yummy in his sleek dark blue Calvin Klein suit. His crisp white shirt was flashing beneath and matched his perfect, straight, white teeth.

He bent down slightly to whisper against my ear, "You look stunning. Do your panties match your shoes?"

I looked down at my black high heels, scoffed and then laughed softly. I squeezed his bicep and gave him a sideways glance, trying to remain coy. "If you're a good boy, maybe you'll find out. So tell me again, who are we meeting for dinner?"

He rubbed his nose into my pulled back hair, kissed the top of my head and then groaned. We'd practiced their names at least a dozen times already. "Jen and Kent, your two old high school friends."

I grinned at him and grabbed his tie, pulling him down for a quick kiss.

"That's right. And what topics are we avoiding tonight?" I asked.

His hazel eyes flashed gold as he stared down into mine. He spoke low, his voice sending little flickers through my body, "Kids, and anything involving you."

I nodded and rewarded him with another kiss, this one a little longer, our lips grazing softly, drawing out into longer kisses. It was interrupted by a man clearing his throat loudly.

I stepped to the side and pulled back when I realized Kent and Jen were standing there staring at us.

Kent was dressed in a suit, he looked handsome but extremely uncomfortable, he kept pulling at his collar. He had a large purple present under his left arm, the silver bow sparkled in the subdued lights of the street.

I pasted on my happy face and hugged Jen. "Happy Birthday, Birthday Girl!" I gave her an extra squeeze and then stepped back.

She smiled softly, it almost reached her eyes, and looked between me and my date. "Thank you. You look great, Elly. Better than I do tonight, don't you think, Ken?"

She looked at her husband and nudged him to get his papabear glare off from Dave.

He didn't even glance at me, avoided looking at me entirely. Had it been a decade ago I would've been offended, but as it was I was used to his avoidance in the presence of others. It was just the way he was since the night we don't ever bring up.

"No, of course not, Jen. Don't be silly. You look terrific," he said with a tiny smile.

She did. She looked sophisticated in her split neck knee-length blue dress. I always admired how she always seemed to look so put together. Even if she showed up at Kent's work after hitting the gym in a t-shirt she would end up looking like an Adidas advertisement. Kent leaned in to press a kiss to her cheek but she pulled back.

"Make-up." She smiled sweetly to play off the blatant rejection of his affections and then nodded towards the door of the fancy Italian restaurant. "Shall we? Our reservation won't keep for much longer."

We walked, single file, into Amici. I felt my shoulders tighten as Dave's warm hand moved to my lower back. I wasn't too keen on his constant need to touch a part of my body any time we were in public, which was always because there was something that was niggling me about him. I just couldn't put my finger on what it was.

After we were seated and the waiter departed with our drink orders, Jen smiled sweetly to us.

"So, how are you guys doing?" Kent asked. I watched as Kent's eyes shifted from me to Dave and then to the silverware on the table. The present was sitting on the table beside Jen, who payed no attention to it.

I spoke up after smiling to Dave, dividing my attention as evenly as I could between my three dinner companions.

"We're good. Dave moved into a those new apartments across from the Town Centre last week. He's on the 15th floor and the view is absolutely amazing..." I paused and took a sip of water, my throat feeling as parched as the desert as I tried to bring some life and cheer to the table.

I felt Dave's eyes on me, and when I glanced at him they seemed to simmer as he watched my lips puckering on the frosty glass.

Jen beamed at us from across the table. "Sounds amazing. We're still over on Bridge Street but you already knew that. Nothing new. I spend all day at home while Ken runs his businesses. It's the life of a rich man's wife, it seems." Jen always dropped the T off of Kent's name. It forever annoyed me, but I always kept it to myself.

Dave laughed softly, "So, do you sit around and watch TV and eat bon-bons all day? That's what stay-at-home wives do, isn't it?"

I laughed softly at the question and shook my head. I was curious what Jen's response was going to be and snuck a glance at Kent, catching him smirking briefly.

Kent spoke up first, "Ordering movies on pay-per-view, going shopping, ordering things on the internet...I think that about covers it, wouldn't you say?" His arm was on the back of her chair as he looked at her.

She frowned a little as she reached over and puckered his cheeks between her fingers. "You forgot cooking, my dear. I make a mean frozen pizza."

Jen winked at Dave and Kent shook his head, his gaze firmly on Jen.

"Oh yes, Mr. P's for the win," he muttered.

Dave gave Kent a once over and shrugged. "Doesn't look like she starves you. How is it having a wife as hot as yours waiting at home for you every night?"

He put his arm around me and tugged me gently against his side. I winced briefly but smiled to cover the discomfort of leaning over the space between our chairs.

"Some day soon I hope I'll have a wife of my own at home." Dave stared down at me and I glanced up to meet his eyes.

He had that look there. A look of longing, of promises. I was starting to feel a bit panicky. I pressed a kiss to his lips and then pulled back.

"It's wonderful. I look forward to it every day when I close up the shop. It's something everyone should wish for. Elly would make a good wife." Kent leaned over to try to give Jen a kiss on the cheek but stopped. "Right, make-up. Excuse me while I go to the restroom." Kent slid his chair out and stood from the table just as the waiter dropped off our drinks.

I watched Kent briefly as he stood up from the table before turning my attention back to Jen.

"What are you and Kent doing this weekend?"

"Well, he has his third shop opening next Saturday so he'll probably be there all weekend to get things set and do the training. So I guess that means I'm free!" She grinned at both of us, looking expectantly.

I looked between Jen and Dave and put my hand on Dave's knee and gave it a gentle squeeze. "I'm busy Saturday too. Booked for two weddings."

Dave sighed, "Right, I forgot. I'll miss you." He leaned down and pressed a kiss to my cheek.

I felt my cheeks color and smiled at Jen. "You're not going to the store opening?"

She shook her head. "What's there for me? Computer nerds ogling my goods and women hitting on Ken who don't deserve his attention? No, I'll keep my jealousy to myself, thanks." Jen laughed softly as my fists clenched together tightly under the table as she left the 'T' off his name.

Kent returned to the table and took his seat once again. "Sorry. What did I miss?" He asked as Jen turned her face to look at him.

"Oh, I told them your new shop was opening. Said you'd be busy."

I noticed Kent's ears were turning a little red and shifted in my seat. His ears only did that when it was cold out or when he was getting angry. It wasn't very cold in the restaurant.

"I see. So not much of anything, then," Kent said.

I glanced at Dave who was looking just as uncomfortable as I was with the marital tension on the opposite side of the table.

I cleared my throat and pointed to the speakers overhead, "Oh, I love this song. I wish I spoke Italian. You speak some, don't you,

Dave?"

Dave received my signal loud and clear and nodded, "A little. Jen, Kent, do you speak any languages?"

The married couple glared at each other for a moment but then Dave's question sunk in and the tension was gone. Jen was the first to answer, she kept her gaze pointed at Dave. "No, I don't speak anything other than English, and I'm bad at that most days. Kent speaks a few, but I don't hear him speaking them much around the house anymore."

Kent cleared his throat as the coloring in his ears was starting to fade. "I speak C ++ and Basic." He didn't wait for the pause to his computer nerd joke, "I also speak French and a bit of Latin." Kent shrugged his shoulders nonchalantly, as if he weren't as amazing as I still knew him to be. As a person, not a man.

"Kent is too smart for his britches. Always has been." I grinned, trying to lighten the mood.

Dave laughed. "Yeah? I went into business because that computer stuff was too daunting."

"For you and me, both." I nudged Dave with my elbow playfully.

"Kent ended up with his Master's in that computer stuff and a minor in Language Arts. I told him he should have been a teacher...I think he would have liked that better."

Kent turned to Jen and smiled coldly. They had this argument before too. Kent saw the dollar signs in Jen's eyes and made every effort to give them to her. Jen ate it up and kept asking for more. "Maybe I should have. I don't know. Some days are better than others, right?" He looked at us for support.

I smiled. "I'm not sure anyone loves their job every minute of it." Dave's fingers captured my right ear and gently starting moving his fingers over it.

"Except you, right, Els?" Dave asked.

I looked at Dave after putting my shoulder to my ear to stop him from stroking it. "Even I have bad days at work."

Kent sipped his tea and then spoke up, "How is the singing treating you, Elly? We've...well, I've been so busy with the new store that we haven't had much of a chance to talk."

That much was true. Their wedding spurred a huge jump in my wedding singing career. I had thought, at the time, that it would be a great way to earn some extra money. Almost a decade later and I was still doing large events along with open mic nights when I wasn't waiting tables, which was my day job. Between the two I had enough to pay the bills and very little time for a social life.

"It's going well. I wish more people would have weddings during the week, but," I shrugged, chuckling softly. "I'll take what I can get. Excuse me, I have to use the ladies room."

Chapter 2

Once alone, I stared at myself in the mirror and pulled out my phone. I groaned as I noted that we'd only been seated for twenty minutes. It felt more like eighty. I freshened up my face, checked my email, and shot Stacy a text.

ME: OMG. THESE BIRTHDAY DINNERS ARE THE WORST!

STACY: ARE U TEXTING AT THE TABLE? RUDE!

ME: I'M IN THE LADIES. HAHA. HAD TO TAKE A BREATHER. JEN IS ALREADY ON HER SECOND COCKTAIL.

STACY: IT'S HER BIRTHDAY. GIVE HER A BREAK.

ME: *ROLLS EYES* WHATEVS. DO I HAVE 2 GO BACK?

STACY: YES! CALL ME LATER! :-*

When I came back there was an odd tension at the table. I sat down and was about to ask what I'd missed when the food arrived. We all ate dinner and made small talk.

When it was time for dessert the waiter came to our table with a gang of wait staff behind him, the chocolate cake slice glittered on the plate, leading the way. They all sang "Happy Birthday" and clapped when it ended. Jen closed her eyes and blew out her candle.

"What did you wish for, Jen?" Kent grinned as he sat back, rubbing his stomach as if he were full, which seemed odd because he'd barely eaten anything. Jen sucked the chocolate from the candle and I couldn't help but wonder if she was trying to seduce Kent or

Dave. Neither would surprise me and I resisted the strong urge to roll my eyes.

"You know Jen can't tell you or her wish won't come true. I think it's present time!" I nodded to the large purple present which I'd wanted to open since I'd seen it.

Jen apparently didn't need further prodding. She grabbed the present and ripped the paper open despite Kent's attempt at speaking up to say something about the gift. He smiled at her excitement of opening the present, purple paper flew everywhere.

Peeking from the box was a slight sparkle. She pulled the dress out and held it up to her chest. The low-cut v-neck was embellished with hundreds of tiny diamonds. Kent was smiling as he watched her.

"Happy Birthday, Jen! It's from Elly and I."

I was about to speak up but held my tongue. I had nothing to do with that gift to Jen and the one in my purse seemed severely inadequate after Kent's extravagant purchase.

Dave whistled. "That's quite a dress."

She examined it and nodded slowly, "Yes...it's uh...something!" I could clearly see the false smile as she looked at me, "What do you think, Elly? Does it look good?"

I nodded with an approving smile, "Yes, it's beautiful." I glanced at Kent whose lips fell slightly at Jen's less than enthusiastic reply.

Jen looked between us, "Thanks, Elly and Kent. Maybe I'll wear it around town tomorrow!" She laughed and then put the dress back into the box, daintily tapping the top once it was secured.

Kent nodded at his wife, "You're welcome. Well. If you guys want to hang out a little more, you can. I need to get home since I have an early start to the day tomorrow. It was really nice of you guys to come out on such short notice." Kent was pretty much just talking to me.

I smiled softly and then turned my glance to Jen. "I wouldn't have missed it for the world." I looked at Dave who nodded at me that he wanted to leave and we stood. "Happy Birthday again. I hope you have a good night," I said as I walked around the table and hugged Jen one last time to seal the friendly relationship for another year.

Dave held his hand out to Kent for a shake, "Nice to meet you,

Kent."

"Nice to meet you too, Dave." Kent returned the handshake.

Jen squeezed me tightly for a moment and kissed me on the cheek. She whispered softly into my ear so that only I could hear. "Have fun tonight."

After those words she picked up the box and moved to stand by Kent. Kent moved around and put his arms around me, surrounding me with his warmth.

"Good to see you as always. Maybe we can do lunch later in the week. That is, if you bring it by work." His words weren't too loud because Jen still turned green if Kent and I spent time alone without her. Although she no longer had anything to fear from me.

The whole year after their marriage I kept my distance, trying to get myself together after the heartache. It took me a long time to be able to be in the same room with him without wanting to burst into tears.

Kent had never pushed for a reason why, but I had made myself scarce with work which was good enough for him as a newlywed man and a brand new entrepreneur.

As their second anniversary rolled around I had finally come to terms with the fact that Kent was a friend. Just a friend. And that's all he would ever be. By their fifth anniversary I finally made him into a eunuch in my mind, and it was so much easier to be around him. After I started waiting tables downtown near Kent's new computer store I brought him lunch. It gave us time to rekindle our friendship in the safe environment of his business.

I grinned and pulled away after a brief two seconds of contact. "If you're lucky. Make me proud, Kent. Be extra nice to your wife."

I winked at Kent and then stepped back beside Dave and waved goodbye. With our goodbyes said we parted ways at the door. Kent walked with Jen towards the SUV and opened the door for her. He gave one last wave to me and then disappeared from view.

I turned my attention back to Dave. "I think I'm going to have to ask for a raincheck for dessert tonight." I pressed a kiss to his lips and then stepped back, taking in his playful pout.

"Alright, that's two desserts that you owe me. I'm very good at keeping records," he said.

I smiled and let my hands drop from his as I took slow, careful steps backwards so my black heels wouldn't catch on anything. "So am I." I winked at him and then slowly walked away, leaving him without a goodbye. Every man loved a little hard-to-get.

Chapter 3

I cursed myself for the third time as the cold wind bit at my exposed goose-fleshed arms. I ate a little too much at dinner and decided to walk back to my apartment instead of taking a cab. I had learned mid-way through college that the key to having a hot body was through moderation and keeping the calorie count down. And the only two ways to reduce the calories were to starve or exercise. I found that I preferred the exercise but as the wind hit me again I was rethinking my decision. Surely skipping breakfast tomorrow would be less painful than this.

I was halfway home when I spotted Kent's SUV parked on the curb in front of Bella, the upscale dress shop that Kent had probably purchased that extravagant dress from. I almost passed by Jen without noticing that she was sitting outside on the black wrought iron bench because I was busily looking for them inside the store.

I heard Jen whisper, "Elly?" I whipped my head around and then came back to sit beside Jen, whose mascara was running, her eyes slightly puffy from crying.

"Jen, hey, why are you crying? What happened?"

I looked over her depleted form, she looked every bit like a human being at that moment and much less like the rich untouchable socialite that she always projected. My hand rubbed over her back to comfort her and I wondered what the hell had happened in the past forty-five minutes to make her look so gutted. And I also wondered where the hell Kent was.

She had a tissue to her nose and mouth and made a little quivering sob, "Ken and I, we're just so miserable. I don't make him happy anymore and I don't know what I can do. He's so distant, he works all the time. I was actually surprised that he even bothered to show up for my birthday dinner this year. We used to have so much fun together. He used to be funny, carefree..."

I just listened, letting her get it all out. There was no use trying to defend Kent, it would appear that I was on his side and honestly, I didn't want to be on anyone's side. This was their marriage, not mine. My aim had always been to be a listening ear.

"And that dress was just ridiculous. Where would I even wear something like that? I've been hinting for months that what I wanted was a vacation, a second honeymoon. And instead he blows our money on a gaudy diamond encrusted dress. He said he wanted me to have something that would match my beauty and worth to him but that was just his cover up. He doesn't want to go away with me. He doesn't want to be alone with me." She started to sob again and I held back a sigh.

This was not the first time I'd heard this complaint from Jen. She didn't seem to understand that Kent was working his ass off for her. She was used to living a certain way and he was trying his damnedest to live up to her expectations. Jen was a smart woman, always had been, and I truly felt she needed something else in her life to distract her so she didn't hold her magnifying glass over Kent and her marriage 24/7.

She'd clung to Kent and made her life revolve around acquiring and keeping him. She used to have school to fill in the times when she wasn't with him. But after college and marriage she just stayed home claiming she wanted to make a nice house for Kent and that she didn't want to quit her career midyear when she finally got pregnant again. The pregnancy never happened and nine years later here we were. Both of them seemed miserable. But as Switzerland I kept my opinions to myself.

I continued to rub her back and looked over my shoulder into the store once more. "Where did he go? Is he inside?"

She let a humorless laugh escape her throat. "No, he ran off, like a coward. Even after bulking up and getting rid of the geeky glasses he still hasn't lost that trait. He still runs away from confrontation."

"He probably just needed some time to cool off. He'll come back for you."

"Maybe he will, maybe he won't. I won't be here to find out. I'm going to spend the rest of my birthday doing something fun."

She straightened up and pushed her long blonde hair over her slim shoulder. I couldn't help but smile. She was an expert at bouncing back.

"That a girl!" I put my hands flat on the bench on either side of me and sat up straight too. She was still about half a foot taller than I was. She turned my way as she dabbed away the runny mascara.

"Elly, why didn't you fight for Kenny?"

I felt my cheeks color. I really didn't want to discuss what I considered to be the most embarrassing time of my life.

I shrugged my shoulders and pasted on a smile, "He didn't want me, Jen. He wanted you. He picked you, over and over again."

I made sure I emphasized that for both our sakes. It was easy to romanticize the past, and think back and remember things that weren't truthful.

"I always thought he wanted you. Sometimes I still wonder if he does." She stuffed the used tissue into her large designer purse and stood up.

I stood up too, "You're just hurt. You'll see things clearly tomorrow. Kent loves you. He adores you. How could he not?" I smiled again and reached out, squeezing her elbow affectionately.

She smiled back and sighed softly, looking at the ground in shame. "I'm sorry, Elly. You're right. You're such a good friend."

She hugged me, tail between her legs so to speak. I smiled for her sake as she pulled back and straightened up, the rich bitch face back on.

"Now for my fun. Do you want to come with?"

"I'd love to but I have to be up early for work in the morning. Drink a Long Island for me." I grinned as I watched her walk around the SUV.

She opened the driver's side and paused, "Will do! Thanks for coming tonight, Elly. I hope to see more of you and Dave. You two look really great together."

She smiled a little, waved and then got in and closed the door. I watched as she pulled away from the curb and sighed heavily. I had one more stop to make and it was going to be too long to walk. When she was out of sight I hailed a cab.

Chapter 4

I paid the taxi driver and got out into the dark evening, shutting the door softly behind me. I looked up, tilting my head back, and stared up at the darkened dilapidated tower that I liked to call Kent's brooding place.

Whatever had gone down with Jen was surely what had brought him here, if he was even up there. I'd bet tomorrow's breakfast that he was. I slowly made my way up the metal ladder to the top of the tower. I stared into the darkness when I reached the top, trying to make Kent's shape out from the rest of the shadows. The breeze that made the trees sway washed over me, and I shivered.

After my eyes adjusted I caught sight of his form. Right on the edge of the tower he sat with his legs dangling over the side. His tie was loose around his neck and his jacket was balled up and resting not far from him looking like a sleeping, disheveled cat. This is where he always came to clear his head. This was where he came to make his decisions and let his anger and frustrations out. I smiled as I remembered the first time he brought me up here. It was nice to have a decent memory regarding losing my virginity because the event itself had sucked so badly.

I stepped forward, coming up behind him slowly. My heels were the only sound aside from the wind which was still blowing past my ears.

"Don't jump. I would be devastated." I hoped my joke would land and sighed when I was unable to get a chuckle from him.

"Jumping is not the hard part, it's the landing at the bottom that sucks. Seconds of freedom and flying, and for what? Pain for the rest of your life? Shouldn't you be off having fun somewhere with Dave?" Kent hadn't looked back at me yet. "Why are you here?"

I sighed softly when I was unable to get a chuckle from him. I sat down beside him carefully. After a fall off a stripper pole a couple of years ago I developed a fear of heights. I dangled my legs over the edge too. I put my hands in my lap and stared at him, my head turned to the side.

"I ran into Jen. So I couldn't possibly have fun knowing that my best friend was probably very hurt because his wife returned his gift."

"If she would have bought that dress herself, she would have loved it." He shook his head and let out a defeated sigh. "I bought it for her and she decided it was too much. I should be able to buy my own wife a gift with the money I work so hard for." The muscles in his jaw worked as his teeth clenched together, a bit of anger showing through his usually calm facade.

"I think maybe she just wants your time," I clasped and unclasped my hands in my lap, unsure of how he would receive my feedback.

Kent nodded his head. "I know that's what she wants. We tried that already. I put one of the guys in charge of each place and I took time off. Without me being there though business was lacking and was dropping off. No people equals no money. Soon she was telling me I needed to be there. Now you can see why I'm such a fucking mess, Elly." Again his head shook back and forth. "We're not doing well, Elly. Not at all."

Kent may have given up but Jen didn't seem like she had just yet. It was up to me to push my friend to fight. He picked Jen as his first kiss, his first girlfriend, his first everything and I wasn't going to let his momentary anger over a dress cause him to do or say something that was going to jeopardize what he built his most of his life to accomplish.

"Maybe not now, but it's obvious that you both still want it to work out. And that's something, isn't it?" I hated seeing them like this. They both needed a push towards each other. Maybe counseling.

He turned his head and looked at me for a long moment. His

eyes were red rimmed and it was obvious that he'd been crying.

"It's just hard, Elly. I work so hard to give her the things she obviously wants, but she just doesn't seem to enjoy it. I...I—," his words broke off as his gaze turned back out towards the city.

This was hard for me too. Seeing him in pain, wanting to comfort him, but refraining. I hadn't touched him for longer than thirty seconds since the night of his bachelor party.

"You're not happy and she's not happy," I swallowed the lump in my throat as I looked at his tear stained cheeks. "You need to do what will make you happy, Kent."

"I just don't want to think about work. I just want to play a video game or watch a movie," he shook his head. "I just want to have some fun for once instead of worrying about everything else."

"Then close your expansion stores and keep the most lucrative one open. Take your life back and let Jen know that X is how much money you're going to make. Then take time to play a video game or watch a movie." I sighed softly, the fight leaving me as quickly as it had come. "I work a lot too, Ken. Two jobs. But I still manage to find time for fun. I'm not sure that this is all her fault."

"I already told her I'd get rid of one and wouldn't open the other. She told me no. I've had offers on the business, but I've turned them down. I've tried, Elly. I have."

"It's your business, Kent. And it's your life. You need to stop letting her steamroll it, if that's what you feel she's doing here."

I watched him, letting him run what I'd said through his mind a little longer. I turned my attention to the city landscape, it all looked so small from up here. Perspective was everything. From my perspective Kent was tired of Jen being unhappy with everything he'd tried to give her. And Jen was tired of feeling alone in her marriage.

Kent sat there for a moment before he finally spoke up, "I got some Mountain Dew at the house and I DVRed an old scary movie. You game?"

I opened my mouth to accept right away but paused. What would Jen think if she came home and saw me with Kent watching a movie on their couch? Would she care? Was she allowed to care?

I was just his friend. But I had told her that I was tired and needed to get home for my early shift tomorrow. And shouldn't Kent be spending this time with Jen to try and work things out?

"What about Jen? Shouldn't you ask her first? She also mentioned to me that she wanted to have some fun tonight. Maybe you two could spend some time together?"

He scoffed. "Then that means she was going to go out with her girlfriends. That means no dudes allowed. Sounds like that clears me to hang out with my best friends. Yeah?"

"....I have to get up early for work in the morning?" I had to try to use the same excuse on Kent as I did with Jen, at the very least. "You should call your other friends instead, like Mike or Paul..."

"It's been too long since I've hung out with you, Elly. Sometimes when you get pulled knee deep into life you forget the important things, like your real friends. I have to get up early too. I have some businesses to sell and some life to recapture. C'mon, I'll even sweeten the deal with a pedicure."

I hesitated. I had purposely not spent time alone with him in any setting outside of his office. My fatal mistake was looking him in the eye. Seeing the hope and desperation there, I couldn't resist any longer. I sighed and turned around, crawling a bit away from the edge before standing up.

"Fine. No toe nail painting, though." Even if I went over to his house, it didn't mean I had to have him touching me. It was basically the same thing as me touching him and it was a very non-platonic thing to do.

"What, don't paint your toenails anymore? You used to bug me about that all the time." Finally he chuckled as he pushed back from the edge and grabbed his jacket. He stood up and moved towards the ladder, waiting for me to join him. I closed the distance between us.

"That was back in high school. I pay someone to do it now," I hated lying to him but it was easier than the truth. I stood next to the ladder and looked down briefly. "You have to go first. If I fall I want you to be there to break it." I smiled innocently to him.

Chapter 5

Kent was starting to come out of his emotional funk.

"Alright, well I guess that will work. I'll make sure not to look up then Miss I'm-Wearing-A-Fancy-Skirt."

I knew he was being serious. He was always proper and gentlemanly, even when we were teenagers. But he probably was just like that with me because he saw me as a friend, like one of the dudes. If I didn't keep reminding myself of that I might let my old feelings resurface. They had to stay buried deep. I didn't want to be hurt like that again.

"You'd better not."

I waited for him to start down and then headed down behind him. Once he was halfway down I screamed, looking down to see if he was going to look up. When he looked up and spotted the black thong under my skirt he blushed, his cheeks burning with his embarrassment. I didn't get to see them for more than a second though before he was looking down at his feet, concentrating on the task at hand.

I grinned at my victory. "You owe me next week's allowance."

"Bah, playing on my chivalry to get money out of me. You never did play fair!" Kent chuckled as he reached the bottom and stepped back to wait for me to come down the rest of the way.

I huffed softly when my heel connected with the ground. "Oh, thank God, I made it! I wish you'd pick a less vertical spot to lick your wounds. Are you going to call the cab or do you want me to?" I already started pulling my phone from my purse, shivering as the wind sent a gust over us.

I felt something sliding over my shoulders. I gazed at the jacket that Kent was no longer wearing and looked at him, his tie was slightly blowing in the breeze.

"Call a cab? We could just walk. It isn't that far."

I pulled the jacket closed in the front and slipped my phone back into my purse. "Thanks. Let's go before my feet fall off."

We walked beside each other, untouching and then I heard him chortle. "Feet fall off. You want a ride?" He pointed to his back with his thumb. "First one's free, then you owe me lunch."

I laughed softly and shook my head, "No, thanks. I'll survive." What was with him wanting to touch me all of a sudden? He went from not even looking at me during dinner to wanting to grab my ass and call it a piggy-back ride. I mentally tried to count how many drinks he'd had. It hadn't been enough to make him drunk.

"Alright, then." He chuckled to himself as we moved on towards the house he shared with his wife. We went over idle small talk, like how my work was going, how he couldn't find anyone to manage a business and soon enough we were walking up the driveway to the large house.

I hadn't been over much except for the occasional dinner party where Jen tried to set me up with her few single male acquaintances. I smiled patiently as I waited for Kent to open the door. I entered the house and looked around, nodding. Everything was different.

"Jen has good taste."

"She's done all the decorating, as you know. I just pay for the stuff." He shut the door behind us. "Just toss the jacket on the coat rack if you want. I'll get us some Dew and meet you on the couch!" For the first time in a long while he seemed really excited, more like the Kent I'd known most of my life.

I put his jacket up as he'd instructed and then made my way into the living room. I sat down on the beautiful yet uncomfortable couch, pulling my shoes off slowly one by one. I let them drop to the floor and pulled my feet up under my skirt. I looked around in amazement. Their living room looked like something out of a decorating magazine. There was nothing but intentional clutter, beautiful art, and expensive furniture. No personal pictures, no dust. Nothing was out of place.

Kent came in the living room with two glasses of that sweet nectar also known as Mountain Dew. I couldn't drink the whole thing, I wasn't a sugar fiend anymore, but I accepted it as he held it out to me. "Thanks."

I smiled as I watched him take a seat next to me and pick up one of the many remotes that had been tucked away in a basket. He turned the TV on and then the DVR player. "I was going to watch it last night, but I didn't get around to it. But now... now it's gonna happen!" I laughed at his excitement. I only ever achieved that level of excitement these days when I was buying a new pair of shoes... or playing with my band.

"You sound like you did when you first watched the Spiderman movie. Your mom kept interrupting your scheduled movie time and it was a whole week before you got around to it, do you remember?" I took a small sip before placing it on the side table closest to me. Oh crap! I grabbed a coaster and lifted my glass, setting it carefully on top so that I wouldn't leave a mark.

"Yeah, I remember. You know Jen doesn't like scary movies? Every time she came in last night I had to cut it off." He drank half of his Dew before putting it aside as well, not bothering with a coaster. I didn't want to see Jen's reaction when she found out.

I stretched my arms overhead and then crossed them, holding myself.

"Oh, I almost forgot." Kent reached between his side of the couch and the side table and pulled out the awful yellow blanket that had been in his school-aged bedroom longer than I had. As he shook it out a pillow fell out onto the floor. He tried to shove it back between couch quickly and offered the blanket to me. "Here ya go."

I leaned forward to make sure I saw what I thought I'd seen and then leaned back, my eyebrow raised, "Have you been sleeping on the couch?"

Chapter 6

Kent grimaced as he picked up the Dew and took a drink.

"Yeah," he said. He took one more drink and returned it to the table by the couch. His eyes were focused on the TV. If he wanted to avoid my questioning stares that was fine by me. I'd still get my answers.

I stared at the TV too and tried to remain casual, "Because you're just so tired when you come home or...?"

"Because Jen and I haven't slept in the same bed in over a month."

I was stunned. Firstly, because it was so easy to get that information out of him and secondly, because he had been sleeping on a couch for a whole month and hadn't told me. I tried not to let my disbelief show. I busied myself by tucking the blanket around me.

"But I mean...It's a big house, why not sleep in one of the other bedrooms?"

His scent slowly surrounded my senses and I tried to resist inhaling deeply. I kept reminding myself it was because his scent was associated with so many memories, it had nothing to do with those old feelings I used to have for him.

"Because it doesn't feel right sleeping in a bed alone is all. I'd much rather crash the couch."

"It's good to know you can sleep just about anywhere...except a—"

A gangly hand popped out unexpectedly and I screamed, covering my face with the blanket. I heard him laugh at me and uncovered my face enough to glare at him.

"You scaredy cat." He casually put his arm around my shoulder and I felt my body tense. "Are you always gonna get scared at the wittle scawry movies?" He teased me as he turned his attention back to the TV.

"Um, yes...I have good survival instincts, that's all. I'll be right back."

I got up off the couch and went to the bathroom. I took the next few minutes to splash some water on my face and try to figure out why I was feeling so weird. It was Kent, he was just being Kent. He was being casual and friendly. There was nothing behind it, never would be.

I looked at myself in the mirror, pointed at my nose and whispered, "Stop being ridiculous! Stop conjuring up fiction in your silly head, Elly. Be. A. Good. Friend."

I exhaled quickly, smoothed out my dress and then left the bathroom. I was only gone for a few minutes before coming back. I pulled the blanket around myself again and stared at the TV as the zombie with the gnarly hand chased a half-naked, big-boobed girl down the street.

The movie was half over and I whispered, pulling the blanket up to my nose, "They're all gonna die..."

"You know how these movies generally work. Most of the time yes, they do." Kent covered a yawn with his fist.

"I always hope they live," I whispered again. I grabbed the blanket from my shoulders and tucked it around him. He looked so tired and so sad. My heart was hurting for him and his marriage woes. "Looks like it's getting close to your bedtime."

"I got enough to finish the movie! I'm not passing out yet, Elly. Don't forget who usually won those late night gaming sessions! It was me because you always passed out."

I rolled my eyes and shook my head. "Yeah, but you're getting old. You don't party long into the night like I do." I grinned as I tucked my hands into the crooks of my elbows and snuggled back against the couch.

"Yeah, whatever. I can run laps around you any day of the week." He chuckled and pushed part of the blanket onto me. "Just try to finish the movie without screaming again and then we'll call it a night. Alright?"

"I don't remember you being so bossy. Being your own boss must have done that to you, BossyPants." I pushed the blanket back onto him.

"I'm gonna wrap you up like a burrito if you don't accept my hospitality in my own house!"

He stuck his tongue out at me and then he flinched and gasped as the zombie attacked the half naked girl unexpectedly while she was finding comfort in the arms of her male counterpart. Kent was blushing as he glowered at me.

I pointed at him, hiding my giggles behind my hand. "What were you saying, Scaredy Kent?"

Kent grabbed the edge of the blanket and twirled it around us and tied it in a knot.

"Yeah, so what. It's a good movie if it gets me to jump! At least I'm not screaming."

I struggled against the blanket and sighed in defeat after a moment of trying to wiggle out of it. The whole right side of my body was touching his and I was reminded at how warm he was. "There is nothing wrong with screaming. God, you're like a bonfire."

"Screaming makes the blood move. As far as being a furnace... yes, I am. I can only sleep with a sheet year round."

Kent didn't seem to think much about our contact. It was all I could think about, him wrapping me up like he used to when we were teenagers, his lips kissing my shoulder, unlike when we were teenagers... I hopped in my seat because of the movie, but held back my scream.

"I think you forget I've known you since before you could walk," I countered.

"I know. You forget how hot my body runs in temperature? You don't remember complaining about being cold in my room and I'm running around in shorts and a t-shirt? Elly..." he sounded disappointed.

I laughed. "Kent..." And then I rolled my eyes, "If I think about it, yes, I remember. But when I think about Kent, my friend, that doesn't usually pop up." Not that specifically. Other things popped up, but not him running around in shorts all the time.

There was a raise of his eyebrow. "Oh yeah? Maybe I've forgotten but you seem to be holding something over my head. Tell me."

I shook my head, "Nothing, I don't think. It's just that when I think of you I just think of nerdy you with glasses and those awful 90's clothes...and a morbid fear of girls." Of wanting to kiss you so hard that your glasses would fall off. And all those nights I'd prayed that you'd notice the parts of me that were round in a sexy, womanly way and not just in your sleep or in a drunken stupor. I kept those thoughts in my head.

"Right. Not Kent who got tired of being picked on and started working out and got rid of the glasses," he frowned, "And I didn't have a fear of girls, just a healthy weariness of them."

"I don't think about how cold your room used to be or all the crusty socks under your bed either..." I bit my lower lip to keep from grinning too wide. His reaction was going to be classic.

He blinked, "When were you looking under my bed!"

My smiled dropped. His face was turning red.

"Well, did you ever wear those frilly pink panties with the bows on them?" he raised his eyebrow, "Yeah, I knew about those. They were sitting on top of your dresser one day when I came over and I pretended not to see them so you wouldn't be embarrassed."

I had an exact idea about what panties he was talking about. I'd bought them on the very off chance that I could get Kent into my plus-sized jeans. I laughed and gasped, pointing at him accusingly.

"I knew you saw them. I was wondering when you'd say something about them. I wear panties like that all the time." I stuck my tongue out at him and wondered if he was going to try to lift up my skirt to see. I scolded myself for even thinking about it.

Kent chuckled. "The good ol'days, right Elly?" For a moment he didn't say anything. "I miss this. I know we're both really busy, but why did we stop hanging out so much?"

Because of Jen. I cleared my throat and reached out from the blanket, grabbing my phone. "It's late, Kent, I should get going…" I wouldn't meet his gaze, I didn't want him to see what was in my eyes. The regret, the guilt for being so jealous, the hurt he'd put there when he'd chosen her over me so many times in the past.

Kent was about ready to say something but something caught his eye and he looked behind me. In the doorway stood Jen, staring at us. Her purse dangled in her hand, her eyelids wide with disbelief, "What the hell is going on here?"

Ken pushed the blanket aside and stood up. "We were just catching up. It's nothing to worry about, Jen."

Jen, however, was more than worried. She was livid. "In our own house, Kent? You'd bring her here to do that?" We could smell the liquor on her breath from across the room.

I stood up quickly and tried to change the subject, "Jen, did you have a good time?" I approached Jen steadily, acting like the innocent party that I was, a smile on my lips.

Jen glared at me. Her eyes were so full of anger and rage that it was actually frightening. My mouth went dry.

"Get out," she spat at me.

Kent approached the two of us from behind, his arms out to embrace his wife. "Jen, calm down. This isn't what you think."

"Kent, she's right. It's late. We all need some rest." I retreated, grabbing my shoes and purse before anything was said that couldn't be forgiven.

"Good night, Elly." It was the last thing that was said to me before I walked out the large door. As I walked away from the house I could hear Jen yelling at him. As I neared the bottom of the driveway I heard Kent fire back, his temper officially lost.

I considered going back but it wasn't my fight, it was theirs. As much as I wanted to protect and defend Kent, it wasn't my place. I put my shoes on and walked down the street, pulling out my phone to call for a cab and text with Stacy as I waited for it to arrive.

ME: HOLY SHIT! I THINK I MAY HAVE JUST BURNED DOWN KENT'S HOUSE.

STACY: WHAT?? YOU BURNED DOWN HIS HOUSE? WHAT DID HE DO?

ME: I MEANT HIS … NOT HIS REAL ONE. HIS MARRIAGE HOUSE. THEY ARE FIGHTING FIERCELY IN THERE.

STACY: OH. I ALMOST PEED MY PANTS. DON'T DO THAT TO A SISTA.

I shivered as the wind battered me some more.

ME: SHIT IT'S COLD OUT HERE. AND DARK… LIONS, AND TIGERS, AND BEARS…

STACY: OH MY! HAHA. STOP IT. SERIOUSLY, WHAT DID YOU DO? DID YOU KISS HIM??

ME: OMG, NO! HE WAS POUTING ABOUT JEN RETURNING HIS PRESENT SO I AGREED TO WATCH A MOVIE WITH HIM. JEN CAME HOME AND WAS PISSED ABOUT IT.

STACY: UGH. SERIOUSLY? SHE'S SERIOUSLY INSECURE. YOU SHOULD'VE KISSED HIM.

ME: STACY! OMG!!! I'M NOT KISSING KENT AND WILL NOT. NEVER AGAIN. HE'S LIKE THE TRIPLE CHOCOLATE TOWER AT GUPPY'S. IT LOOKS REALLY GOOD, TASTES REALLY GOOD FOR THE MOMENT, BUT ONCE IT SETTLES YOU REGRET IT IMMEDIATELY AND YOU NEVER WANT TO EAT IT AGAIN.

STACY: … KEEP TELLING YOURSELF THAT.

The cab pulled up to the curb and I said goodnight to Stacy. I looked at their house as I was driven away. It looked picture perfect on the outside.

Chapter 7

A week after the big fight I stopped by Kent's office with a big greasy cheeseburger and a large order of fries in hand. I hadn't heard anything from either of them and I was anxious to hear what had happened. Unless it involved sex, and then I definitely didn't want to know.

"Your favorite delivery girl is here!" I set it on top of his keyboard and sat down in the chair in the corner of his office after clearing it off.

Kent looked ragged. His shirt was wrinkled and his hair was more of a mess than usual. "Ah, just what I needed. Food." He didn't even freak out that I'd put the food on the keyboard like he would have once upon a time. Something was definitely wrong.

I whistled low. "You look like shit. What happened with Jen? Did she forgive you yet?" Please don't talk about sex. Please don't talk about sex...

"We're, uh," he paused to stew on the words. He took that moment to take a large bite of the burger and a squirt of sauce dribbled down his shirt. "Oh c'mon!" He shook his head as he pilfered over his desk and found a napkin to wipe his face and shirt with.

I watched him procrastinate for a moment and quickly tired of waiting for his answer. I reached out and grabbed a computer part that was laying around and chucked it at his forehead. It missed, my aim slightly too high, and sailed over his head, hitting the wall behind him. "You're what?!"

He frowned at me. "Jen still doesn't want me in the house. As you can see I'm sleeping in my clothes and if you go to the back room, you'll see there's a cot in there. Does that answer your question, Ms. Patience?"

"Is she mental? I'll go talk to her after my shift lets out. This is crazy. Like a new level of crazy." I looked down at the floor. I couldn't believe what I was hearing. Jen kicked the man out of his own house? He'd paid for that. If anyone should've not been sleeping out of the house it should've been Jen.

"I just deal with it like I always do. You shouldn't have to get involved, Elly." He sighed as he sat the burger down on the table and wiped his fingers on the napkin. He stood from the chair went into the back room and returned. When I looked up he was wearing a new shirt. He must've changed it while I was planning exactly how involved I was going to get.

"But the fight was directly about me. I just want to make sure she's clear that nothing happened and would never happen between you and me."

"She won't hear it from me. She thinks we've been knocking boots for years. She tells me I never loved her and that I've always been in love with you." He shook his head as he took his seat once more.

I couldn't help but burst into laughter. I shook my head and covered my mouth, trying for a good minute or two to get myself together. Kent ate some fries while he waited. "That's ridiculous!" I blurted.

"That's what I said. She didn't want to listen to anything I had to say. All she kept saying was that she wanted a divorce," the words seemed to fall out of his mouth before he could stop himself. He immediately looked like he regretted letting that cat out of the bag.

That definitely stopped the laughter. I swallowed visibly, my eyes on Kent. "Wow. Is that what you want too?" I asked, softly.

"I don't know, Elly. I don't like confrontation, but I believe in fighting for things. I just, I don't know anymore. She's become more distant. I..." Kent pushed the chair back away from the computer.

I nodded, he needed a push and I was going to give it to him. It was clear in his appearance that he was distraught at the thought of losing his wife.

"So you'll fight for her. You can win her back, Kent. How long until you close the other stores?"

"One is already under contract and the other I'm in negotiation for."

I checked my watch. "That's good." I looked at him and smiled. "You'll figure this out. And if you need me, you know my number. I've gotta get back, my lunch break is almost over." That meant that soon the dinner crowd would be coming in. As well as my biggest tips of the day.

Kent nodded his head. "Yeah, I'm a smart guy. It'll get figured out." He stood from the chair and before I knew what was going on he hugged me. "Thank you, Elly. It means a lot."

I was like a brick wall in his arms and awkwardly patted him on the back. The physical contact with him was making me anxious. "Anytime." I pulled away and slunk out of the shop.

* * *

Another week went by and I still hadn't heard anything about the outcome of the huge marital fight. I hadn't wanted to text or call either in case it was bad. I was missing teasing Kent so I dropped by his store, his lunch in my hand.

I stepped into his office and dropped the warm contents in the middle of his keyboard. His eyes were on me as soon as I stepped in.

I didn't think it was possible but he looked even worse than he had last week. "Dude. What the hell happened to you?" I asked as I sat down in the chair across from his desk.

He frowned as he considered my question, "What are you talking about?"

I scoffed, "Are you kidding? When was the last time you looked in a mirror? Jen seriously let you leave the house like that?"

"Jen doesn't really give a shit anymore."

It was my turn to frown. "What do you mean?"

He picked up the burger and brought it to his lips to take a bite and mustard dripped down the front of his white shirt. "Sonofabitch," he growled. He took a big bite and as he chewed he stood up and pulled his shirt off, revealing his chiseled bod. I pulled my eyes away, choosing to stare at the wall instead as I wondered what he'd meant by that.

Were he and Jen finished? Was that even possible? What would Kent's life look like without Jen in it? Without her weight around his neck he might actually start to enjoy his life again. But I was jumping to conclusions.

When I looked up again he had on a clean shirt and was chewing like a man who hadn't eaten in days. I waited as long as I could to pester him but his lack of answers was frustrating me. "Oh my god, Kent! Tell me what happened!!" My palms were pounding on his desk rapidly.

He swallowed and then wiped at his mouth with a napkin. "Jesus. Can't a man eat in peace?"

"Yes...after said man tells his friend what happened."

He sighed and sat back, setting the burger down. "Fine. We had a huge fight and she demanded a divorce. Happy now?"

"Divorce?" I was shocked. Too shocked to ask all the important questions. Like, did he want a divorce? Was he happy or sad about it? Were they going to try to work it out? Who was going to get the house?

"Yeah. Guess my monogamous, hard working ass wasn't enough for her."

"I..." I was still at a loss for words. My heart was thudding in my chest as I stared at him. He picked up his burger and started to eat again. His mind having had a whole week to wrap itself around the situation. Was he really going to throw away a nine year marriage just like that?

My phone sang to me, letting me know I needed to get my ass out of Kent's chair so I could get back to work. "Shit. I've gotta go. Where are you staying?"

"Here."

"Here?" I shook my head as I made my way to the door, "No, no. You need to find a place to live, Kent. ASAP. I'll help you go look for a place tomorrow, okay? It's my day off. Clear your calendar."

When I turned around Kent's head was on his folded arms and his shoulders were shaking. I rushed over to him and put my hand on his shoulder. "Kenny...come on, it's going to be okay."

He didn't look up, he just put his large, warm hand on top of mine. I squeezed his shoulder and then slipped my hand from his. "You come by my place tonight, I've got a nice couch that has your name written all over it."

He looked up, his eyes red and damp, "Thank you, Elly."

"That's what friends are for," I smiled down at him as I ruffled his hair gently. "I've gotta go. I'll see you later." I blew him a friendly kiss and then booked it back to work.

Chapter 8

After work I checked my phone for messages and saw a text from Jen.

Jen: Kent is angry. I don't know where he went. I think he might do something stupid.

I frowned at my phone. Surely Kent wouldn't kill himself. Jen was probably just over-reacting and being Jen. Or maybe it was her ego making her say to me that he would be so distraught about losing her that he'd kill himself. I sighed as I texted her back.

Me: We need to talk. Meet me for lunch tomorrow?

I dialed Kent's cell, walking the short distance back to his shop while I waited for him to answer.

"You've reached Kent. I can't pick up right now, but if you leave a message I'll get back to you." The recording played on his voicemail. Soon after the voicemail my phone tweeted signaling a message from Jen.

JEN: OF COURSE. TIME AND PLACE?

I peeked into the shop only to find that it was empty. All the lights were off and Kent's SUV wasn't anywhere to be seen. I frowned as I quickly made my way to my apartment. Maybe he was there. I changed my clothes when I didn't see him and then called a cab. I returned Jen's text while we drove.

Me: The place that only serves the salads. 11am.

She knew the place I was talking about, it was the usual place we ate lunch whenever Jen needed to discuss Kent, which was almost always exclusively around major gift-giving holidays.

The cab pulled up to Kent's tower and I got out. I looked up, trying to see if I could spot him. I was dressed for the occasion this time, in spandex running pants, a sweatshirt of our alma-mater, and athletic shoes. I stuffed my phone into the front pocket of my hoodie and started to climb up.

Kent was at the edge, like always. His hands rested on the floor of the tower on either side of himself. I stopped a couple feet away from him, my hands stuffed into my front pocket. "Don't jump. I would be devastated."

"You'd be the only one, Elly." He took in a breath and let it out slowly. "Did you know Jen was sleeping with Dave?" I was pretty sure I hadn't heard him right.

"I...what?..." I blinked. I hadn't broken things off with Dave, we'd seen each other almost every night for the past week.

"I went to the house to try and work things out. When I showed up there was a car there. I thought nothing of it, of course. I went to the door and knocked. When Jen came to the door she just told me to leave. I simply inquired about the car and she flipped out. So, needless to say, I pushed the door open kind of hard and Dave was standing there in the kitchen. When I confronted them both about it, well..." He paused for a beat before continuing, "Apparently it's been going on for a little while now."

All the past feelings came rushing over me, overwhelming me. Jen had taken another man from me. Despite her being married and my being single. Despite the quasi-friendship I'd thought we'd built over the last nine years. She'd taken another guy out from under me. She was my Jolene. I turned away from Kent and started towards the ladder.

I heard Kent scramble up from the ground. He came up behind me and put his hand on my shoulder to stop me from running. "Elly, I didn't want to have to tell you this way. But it's hard to find out that it's the both of us this has happened to."

I stepped back from his touch, tears clouding my eyes. "Don't. Please, don't. I can't... I can't do this right now. I can't be your shoulder to cry on. Go stay at a hotel tonight." I turned back to the ladder, climbing down before I was unable to see my feet. He didn't try to follow me, and I was grateful for that little grace. What the hell was she thinking sleeping with my boyfriend? What the hell was wrong with her? Why did she have to swoop in and take every man I was interested in?

I ran until my lungs were on fire, until my brain could think of nothing except how much pain I was in.

* * *

I had cried so much last night that my eyes were slightly swollen. I kept my large shades firmly in place as I stepped into the salads place. After today I would never again step inside of it. I had a feeling today was going to be a bit dramatic. Jen was long overdue for a verbal smack down and I was finally confident and angry enough to give her one.

She smiled at me as I sat down across from her. I returned the smile, I could play the rich bitch "everything is kosher" game too. If she wanted to smile at me as if she hadn't been backstabbing me for the past three months, or longer, who knows which other of my boyfriends' she'd slept with, I would gladly play along.

The waiter was prompt, offering me another moment of stalling. I ordered a glass of champagne and then put my napkin on my lap. She lifted her flawlessly manicured brows and smiled as she took a sip of her water, "Are you celebrating something?"

"Yep. I'm finally going to do something today that I've been waiting for over a decade to do. It's going to be epic and I'm probably going to feel magnificent after I've done it."

Jen set her glass down and laughed, "You're finally getting a colonic?"

Oh my god, she was clueless. How could she sit there and act so casual with me when she'd been fucking my boyfriend? I tried to keep the anger from my face as I returned the smile.

"No, that's an exit only. But Dave tells me that's not the case with you." I sipped the water sitting at the table, keeping my tone friendly despite the fire I was feeling inside.

She raised her eyebrows in surprise and then scrunched them

up as her angry face arrived, "Excuse me?"

"Oh, we're going to pretend like you aren't screwing my boyfriend behind my back? How many other men have you fucked in your marriage bed? I'm just curious. Maybe you should have your own reality TV show. That was always a dream of yours, wasn't it?"

She laughed, "Elly, dear, you're being ridiculous. Where did you hear this nonsense from?"

"Your husband, of course. He said he walked in on you and my shirtless boyfriend in his living room."

"Was that before or after you fucked my husband?"

I gripped the arms of the chair tightly so I wouldn't slap her across her plastic face. "Don't you dare degrade my relationship with Kent. As far as I know he has been completely faithful to you while you've been screwing around behind his back." Eyes and ears were turning in our direction but I was too angry to care. Fuck the decorum thing. I was starting to see red.

"Please, Elly. Drop the innocent act. I know that you have always had feelings for Kent. You're still holding a grudge with me because he picked me over you."

"Yes, I hate that he picked you. I always have. But I tried to be decent about it. I stayed true to who I was and I was never anything but nice and kind to you. For ten years I've helped you pick out thoughtful gifts for him, I've helped you plan surprise vacations, video games, menus to please him. I have listened to you complain about him, his workaholic ways and I always bit my tongue, as a friend would do, when what I really wanted to tell you was that you are a self-centered, materialistic, whiney-ass self-centered bitch. I didn't make a move on your husband because I cared about the vows you took with each other, because he loved you. But you fucked that all up now. Maybe now is my chance. And if he becomes mine you will never be able to have him again. You fucked up big time." My champagne arrived and I swigged it down, Jen was staring at me, a little dazed by my outburst. I set my glass down and stood up. I looked down at her shocked and appalled face, "Oh, and did I mention I think you're a whore?" And then I turned on my heel and sashayed out of there.

Chapter 9

A few days after the blow up with Jen I finally heard from Kent. I was getting ready for work when I heard the tweet from my phone.

KENT : HEY. I'M CLOSING UP SHOP TOMORROW. HOW ABOUT WE HAVE SOME LUNCH?

I set the phone down as I put the finishing touches on my eye make-up. Did I want to have lunch with him? Yes and no. After all that shit went down with Jen I was halfway curious to ask about her, to see if she'd come crawling back with her pointed tail between her legs. But as it was I was busy tomorrow, so I was off the hook.

ME: CAN'T. I'M WORKING TOMORROW.

I put the phone down and as soon as I did it tweeted again. I felt a little bad for not picking it up right away but I was going to be late for work if I didn't hustle. After putting on my shoes I looked again.

KENT: WHAT ABOUT AFTER WORK THEN?

ME: I HAVE BAND PRACTICE. WE HAVE A GIG THIS WEEKEND.

I stood up and stuffed my phone into my purse. As I was walking out of my building I heard the tweet.

KENT: IS THERE ANY TIME IN YOUR BUSY SCHEDULE TO ALLOW ME TO COOK DINNER FOR YOU?

ME: I'LL LET YOU KNOW.

I stuffed the phone back into my purse and walked quickly

down the couple of blocks to the restaurant.

I was halfway through my shift when I looked up and noticed that Kent was sitting at one of my tables. When I realized it was him my smile faded a little. It wasn't that I wasn't happy to see him, I was, I just... I didn't enjoy being bombarded at work. I pushed my smile to be brighter and leaned against the seat opposite him. "Hey Kent, what are you doing here?"

"I figured that since you were busy with work today that I'd just come get some lunch. That way I could eat and see you. Kill two birds with one stone!" He smiled at me warmly and I looked down briefly, feeling the embarrassment of not feeling so glowing towards him.

I looked back to him, "Sounds good. So what can I get you for lunch?" I looked away for just a moment as I checked my other tables, trying to keep myself in work mode.

"Think I'll go for a chicken caesar wrap with potato salad. Sweet tea to drink." He offered me a grin as he handed over his menu. I took it gently, winked at him and then pushed off the booth. "No problem. I'll be right back with your tea." I felt his eyes on me as I made my rounds. I put tea in front of him and smiled, "Anything else I can get you while you're waiting?"

"Yeah, how much extra does a hug from a best friend cost?" He took a sip from his tea and then slid it in front of him on the table.

I smiled softly as I gazed at his tea. I glanced around and then whispered, "I can't hug you here, if I hugged you I'd have to hug every other guy who asked. The older guys think it's still 1950 and that it's still acceptable to ass-grab the help."

"Fine. Guess I'll just deduct a little from your tip then." He winked at me playfully. "Go on, I'm good. I just wanted to see you, even if it was just in passing since you're so busy."

I rolled my eyes. "I wasn't expecting a tip anyway. Best friends eat free. Your lunch is on me. Your food should be out in a couple of minutes." I smiled, winked and then turned around, walking quickly to my other tables to make up for the time lost speaking to Kent. I heard him chuckling softly and felt his eyes on me.

I brought Kent his food and then went about with my other

customers, schmoozing as necessary to get the most tips. When I stopped back at Kent's table he was halfway through his lunch. "Everything okay?"

He nodded with a smile, "Food is good as always."

"Can I put in some dessert for you?"

"Nah, better not do dessert." He pat his flat stomach. "I haven't worked out in a few days, but thank you none the less."

I rolled my eyes, "Doesn't show. What the hell have you been doing with yourself?"

"Playing video games, reading, leaving work early..." he shrugged his broad shoulders, "I found someone to manage the store so I don't have to be there nearly as much."

"Working out would make you feel better, you know. Get your confidence back up so you can find your next wife."

He rolled his eyes and grinned. "So, I know you're busy, but if you could find yourself with some free time in the next few days, we should work out."

"Maybe. I can run laps around you now." I smiled sweetly at his smug face.

"Sounds like a challenge. Like I said, when you get some free time and you're feeling froggy, then we'll see." He winked at me and I only grinned wider.

"Don't hold your breath for me to feel...froggy." I laughed at him, who said that? What did that even mean? I glanced around at my other tables.

"I'll let you get on with work. Don't forget about me," he said.

"Never," I said as I saw him pulling bills from his back pocket and shook my head. "No way." I grabbed the bills that he placed on the table quickly and shoved them against his rock hard chest. Not that I was feeling him up or anything.

He grabbed the bills from me and stuffed them into the little pocket in the front of my half apron and I froze, his hand so near... my core. He didn't seem phased in the least, just like always. "Later, Elly." He grinned as he walked away from me towards the exit.

I got my wits back about me when he was almost there. I

cupped my hand and yelled, "This isn't over!" And then I quickly got back to work because I noticed my manager at the bar, glaring in my direction.

Chapter 10

I groaned as my alarm went off at five am. What the hell was I thinking? I slapped it hard and then got dressed for my run. I wasn't going to get dressed but then I remembered that I had set my alarm to kick Kent's ass in a friendly competition. The last time I'd beat him at something had been my 16th birthday and it was high time I did it again.

After I'd had my morning Joe I called him from my phone. He picked up after a couple of rings.

"Morning, sunshine. What you want this morning?" His voice was groggy, still filled with sleep. I grinned at the thought of interrupting his beauty sleep.

"Ribbet. Get your ass out of bed and meet me at Slater Park in ten minutes." I hung up and walked briskly there, already warm by the time I arrived.

I popped my earbuds in and started stretching while I waited for his SUV to pull into the parking lot. I closed my eyes as I pulled my chest to my outstretched leg. Today was the day. I could feel it. Today was the day I finally bested Kent. I felt a tap on my back and I jumped up and spun around quickly. Kent's grinning face was there. I pulled out my earbuds and punched him playfully on his chest. "Jerk! I almost peed my pants." It's true, I almost did.

"Look, it's not my fault that you're such an easy target." He snickered as he stretched. "So what's the plan this morning? A brisk run?" It was my turn to grin.

"Yep. Run 'til we drop since you think you can outlast me. Hope you got some good tunes on there." I was a winner damnit, even if I had to cheat a little. I pushed him to ruin his stretch and then started at a slow jog, warming up.

"Sounds like—HEY!" I looked back to see him right himself and jog after me. "Trying to cheat already I see." He chuckled as he slid his earbuds into his ears.

I did the same and after the first lap around I increased my pace. He kept up with me but stayed behind me just a little. I wondered if it was to check out my form, and call me out on something that I was doing wrong. But as the hour passed by he'd said nothing.

He jogged up beside me and I pulled one earbud out, my breathing still very even. He did the same. If anything was going to give out first it was going to be my leg muscles. "Tired of staring at my ass already?" I teased him, hoping he'd blush. "Give up already, you know you want to."

"I've rather enjoyed staring at your ass. But I think it's time you stared at mine for awhile." I grinned as I watched him push a little harder until he was a good three feet in front of me. He was sweating a bit but I didn't see this ending anytime soon. My legs were going to be yelling at me all night but it was going to be worth it.

I let him stay in the lead for the next hour and then I joined him. "You're looking a little wet, Kenny. Ready to tap out yet?"

"You're not so dry yourself, Elly. Maybe you should go hit the shower."

"Only after you tap out, Kenny-poo." I jogged ahead and put my earbuds back in. My poor jogging playlist was starting to get stale.

A half hour later I looked back. He was walking but didn't seem like he was ready to drop. I frowned. He was going to let me win? "Come on, Kent! Don't you dare puss out! I want to beat you fair and square!!"

His smile was back and I felt a smile on my lips too. "Fine." He slowly closed the distance between us, "You want to beat me fair and square, then out run me!" The last few feet he gained in speed and I knew this was it. I increased my pace slowly, not full out running just yet. I was trying to push away the negative thoughts in my head, I was a winner! I was a winner!

He raced ahead but I kept pushing. I couldn't give up. I had to prove to myself that he wasn't better than me. His opinion of me didn't matter as much as my opinion of myself. My opinion was the one that mattered and I thought I was a badass and a winner! The Elly-phant that Kent knew most of his life couldn't do this, but I could. I wasn't her anymore.

I saw him falter, his legs not getting enough oxygen. He bent over and I ran past him, I slowed slowly and then bent over, huffing trying to catch my breath. When he finally came over, huffing himself, I smiled, hands on my hips. "I told you... I could run... circles... around you..."

"Fine...you... win." We walked together back towards the parking lot.

As we went up the hill I smacked his ass as I sped by. "Maybe next time." I heard him laugh behind me. But when I saw what was awaiting us I paused.

"Yeah, maybe, next time, Elly." He nearly bumped into me as I continued to stare as Jen and Dave climbed out of his shiny black BMW. My win gave me big balls. I continued my walk towards the cars, speaking loud enough for Jen to hear.

"Well, well... fancy seeing you two here. And in the light of day. Must feel different."

Jen grabbed Dave's hand and tugged him towards the path. "You both are in desperate need of a shower. We can smell you from here." Dave let himself be tugged along but avoided eye contact with either of us.

I cupped my hands around my mouth and yelled, "We'll be sure to do that. Together! Enjoy your morning stroll!" I watched Jen's shoulders freeze and I grinned to myself. The feeling of wanting to key Dave's car was very much nagging at me but I pushed it away. I was a winner. Winners didn't need to key their ex's cars. I turned to Kent, and smiled sweetly, "Well, thanks for the exercise. I need to get home and shower. My shift starts soon."

"You really know how to dig your nails in, Elly." He looked

from me to our exes and then shook his head. He looked back at me and put his arm around me which I promptly shrugged off. "Since we're both sweaty it doesn't matter. You gonna have any time later?"

"It still matters!" I laughed and shook my head. "No, working the lunch shift and then I need to sleep before my gig tonight. First gig outside of a planned event, it's pretty exciting!" I grinned, I couldn't help it. It was pretty damn exciting. And it was about time. Singing at weddings and bar mitzvahs only got so good. Singing at The Drink tonight was a step up in our music careers.

Kent chuckled, "I'm excited for you, Elly. You'll have to let me know how it goes. I'll be waiting with baited breath!"

Part of me was a little let down. He never watched me sing. He never asked to come to anything, he never asked me to sing for him. It was what I loved the most in life and he didn't seem to have any interest in it. Damnit, Elly! You're a winner! It doesn't matter what he thinks.

"Okie dokie!" I smiled and started to walk away and then turned around and pointed at him. "Oh!" He turned around from his car to smile, eyebrows raised, "You're invited to my birthday party next weekend! Don't forget about that. I'll text you the details!"

He chuckled, "Well I'd hope I'd be invited. Just keep me updated and I'll be there, alright?" He winked at me and then opened his car door. "You sure you don't want a ride? I've got towels to put down on the seats."

I shook my head, "Nope. Jen wasn't lying. We stink bad. I'm just a couple minutes away." I gave him one more wave and then walked to my apartment. It was going to be a long day walking around on overtired legs but it had been worth it.

Chapter 11

I arrived at the gig that night with a smile on my face. My band was mostly there. Bryan and James were tuning their instruments and, as usual, Rio was late. I sighed as I came up to the stage. Bryan's eyes seemed to linger a little too long on my exposed cleavage and the sex goddess inside me squeed.

"Where is Rio?" I asked.

Bryan's eyes met mine and he grinned his hot lopsided grin. It was the same lopsided grin that had won us this audition. The girl's dad owned the bar and shoved us to the top of the call list after he'd flashed her with it at her best friend's wedding a couple weekends ago.

"He had to drop his girl at her mom's house. He's on his way now."

I nodded and then pointed over my shoulder to the bar. "I'm going to get some water, you guys want anything?"

They both responded in unison, "Beer." They glanced at each other and grinned.

When I came back with the drinks, balancing them expertly in my hands, Rio had arrived and was busily setting up his drums.

"Look who made it!"

I teased Rio a lot. He was like my big brother. He was always, always fending off any guys who tried to drunkenly pick me up after an event. It wasn't too often but he had saved me a few times in the past nine years we'd been together as a band.

He let out a gruff caveman grunt. "I'm here, dammit. It's not my fault Stacy's damn car got stuck on the damn freeway during damn rush hour."

I fought back a giggle and pointed at him, "Hey! Don't bad mouth my friend," I said. He grumbled something unintelligible as he warmed up his drumming arms.

"Our first bar gig. I'm so excited!" I squealed. The boys stared at me and I grinned proudly. I handed out the setlist and then tugged at the bottom of my dress. "Here goes nothing!" I turned around and announced us to the buzzing bar. Then we played.

The gig went off without a hitch, we were perfect, and the crowd seemed to love us. The proprietor even asked us to come back next month. And to celebrate I decided we should all pack up and go get shit-faced at a different bar.

Rio grumbled. "I can't, Elly. Gotta go chauffeur my girl in the morning. We'll have to raincheck it."

James nodded and shrugged. "I got work tomorrow."

Bryan was looking at his guitar and I frowned, he probably wasn't going to go without the other two. He avoided being alone with me at all costs. I think it was leftover from when he was dating Siobhan. She was super jealous and made sure he called her every half an hour and if he was alone with me in any capacity she had a bitch-fit. I was glad to see him get out of that chokehold of a relationship.

"I'll go with you, Elly." He looked up and smiled softly.

"Really?" I grinned and then hugged him. It felt...good. I felt my cheeks flaring up and I pulled away, his hand reluctantly let me go.

"Yeah. Rio, cool if you give James a lift?" Bryan asked.

Rio nodded and looked between Bryan and I. He narrowed his eyes at Bryan but didn't say anything. I rolled my eyes. Bryan wasn't going to put any moves on me. Big Brother Rio had nothing to worry about.

* * *

Bryan and I arrived at Red, a swanky bar downtown, just when the after-dinner crowd was dying down. He insisted we sit at a booth.

I scooted in and looked around, noting the stares from the other customers, the ladies were in designer dresses and the men were in suits.

I glanced at Bryan. "I think they realize we aren't one of them."

He laughed, "Yeah, we may be the help now but things can change. Especially for you, Elly. I think you're going to go places. You're too good for us."

I blushed and rolled my eyes to play it off. "Please. I'm average at best." He clasped his hands together loosely on his side of the table and stared at me. I felt his eyes trying to bore into mine and I shifted nervously. "What?"

"I don't understand why you don't see what everyone else can."

I dropped his gaze and looked down at my low cut red sequin dress. "I see a flashy waitress with a decent voice." I shrugged and looked back, meeting his gaze. It caused my body to heat.

"And I see a beautiful but insecure woman. A woman who lights up the room when she walks into it. A woman who sings like an angel. A woman who..." He stopped and then ran his hands through his hair. When his head came back up he shook it, smiling. His friend facade was back on.

"A woman who what?" I scooted closer to him and leaned forward slightly. I didn't want to miss the other wonderful thing he was going to tell me. I was insecure and I wanted to soak it up. Put it in my "Elly is the Best" box in my mind which was already fuller than normal due to the awesome gig we'd just had.

He avoided my gaze for a few moments and then finally met it. "A woman who I very much want to kiss."

I felt my core melt and stayed still, afraid he'd bolt if I made any moves. "So do it..." I whispered. This was bad, dating a bandmate was bad. If the relationship went sour, and it almost always did, it would hurt the band dynamics. But he wanted to kiss me and God help me, I wanted to kiss him too. Not because I thought he was going to be the man I married but because I needed to feel wanted. Dave had only pretended to want me. And his philandering still stung, especially because it'd been Jen that he'd chosen.

I forced my mind back into the present though Bryan was achingly slow, as if expecting me to stop him. He leaned forward slightly, put his hand on my cheek and then after several long seconds of staring in my eyes he touched his warm lips to mine. It was a gentle kiss at first and then it turned to a searing hot brand. His hand moved to my hair and his grip tightened there. He pulled my head closer as I put my hand on his thigh. Our lips mashed together and then broke apart, the milliseconds when they were apart made the tension that much greater and forced us to touch lips again and again.

We made out in that booth for a solid ten minutes and then he pulled away. "Want to go back to my place?" he asked, sex in his blue eyes. I nodded, I wanted a rebound and I wanted it now. He smiled and then softly kissed my nose.

In the car after our roll in his bed I realized just how hysterical he was. It was refreshing being around someone who had no qualms about singing at the top of his lungs. Belting out a song when smiling is the funniest thing ever. He even did some mean air guitar, barely missing several parked vehicles in his passionate air solos. My sides were aching by the time he stopped in front of my rundown apartment building. He ducked to get a good look at the place and shook his head, "Good God, Elly. You need to hit the big time, you deserve better than this place."

I smiled and squeezed his knee. "I'm working on it." I leaned over to kiss him goodnight but he put his hands on my cheeks before our lips touched.

"Night, Elly."

"Night, Bryan." I whispered softly.

As I walked to the front door of my building my mind replayed all that had happened that night. I smiled to myself. I kicked Kent's ass this morning. I cleared $300 in tips at work. I had my first real gig in way too long. It had been a great day.

Chapter 12

My birthday was next weekend and I still had to secure a place. I'd contacted Bubbles and they assured me that my guests would all be allowed VIP access for the evening. I told them the party drink had to be pink. And made sure there were peanut M&Ms, my favorite, on every table.

I multi-texted the guys and asked if they'd play the party and they agreed to rock the pants off all my friends. I sent out a massive e-vite and by the week's end I had 62 yes's and 35 maybe's.

My 30th birthday party was going to rock! I grabbed my phone and texted Kent. I hadn't heard from him since that day we went running together a couple of weeks ago.

ME: HOPE YOU'RE GOING TO BE ABLE TO MAKE IT TONIGHT. MISS YOU. -E

I stuffed my phone into my purse and headed out. The party was in full swing thanks to my late arrival. I slowly worked my way to the bar, greeting and thanking my friends as I moved through the crowded space. Bryan, Rio, and James were on the little stage in the corner doing an awesome job keeping everyone entertained. I was a little disappointed that I hadn't run into Kent yet but I figured he would probably show up towards the end. He didn't like parties or crowds. He usually only went when Jen or I made him go. Hers was one face I wasn't going to missing this year.

The boys took an intermission and the Pussycat Dolls

'Buttons' played over the house speakers. A few ladies from the gym grabbed my hands and pulled me onto the dance floor so we could do the dance routine. It was slightly racey and fun. At the end of the song we were laughing and ready for a drink. I didn't have to go far because Bryan found me and handed me my special pink birthday drink. He leaned in close and spoke into my ear, "Happy Birthday."

I grinned as I took the drink and leaned back to get a look at him. He was wearing his sexy jeans and a black button down short sleeved shirt. He looked good enough to sink my teeth into. I leaned close so I could talk into his ear, "Thanks for keeping the crowd warm."

"Anything for you," Bryan said.

"How many Elly's have you had tonight?" I turned so he could talk into my ear.

"None. I only want one Elly and she's here now." He waggled his eyebrows and I chuckled. He was smooth, I had to give him that.

A co-worker pulled at my arm and I winked at Bryan before being whisked away. I sipped my drink as I worked the room some more.

Half an hour later I was standing by the bar when the boys took the stage again. There was a poofing sound as Bryan tapped on the mic. All eyes turned on him and slowly the crowd turned to a murmur. "Hey everybody! Thanks for coming out to celebrate the birth of our wonderful Elly..."

The crowd hooted and clapped. I blushed and rolled my eyes, my friends couldn't help but to praise me, especially on my big day.

"I um...I've had the pleasure of working with Elly for two years now and in those years I've seen her at her best, which as most of you probably know, is when she's on stage. There is an energy that flows from her when she's in her element. And I've seen her at her worst, like that time she puked all over my shoes and my guitar because she ate that terrible sushi at the Keller wedding." The crowd laughed and I covered my face with my hands in shame. "She's become a great friend and...well," the rest of the band was behind him and got ready to play, "This song is for her. Happy Birthday, Elly." He grabbed his guitar and strapped it on. He nodded to the drummer and the song started.

The chords to my favorite Sister Hazel song, 'All For You', started playing and I let out a loud whoop.

I was all smiles until my attention was drawn away by a tall man dressed in a dark silk suit who'd touched my elbow softly. It took me a minute to recognize that it was Kent. We exchanged smiles and he held a small box to me. He leaned in close so I could hear him over the band and my friends singing along.

"Happy Birthday, Elly," Kent said.

I smiled and took the box, pulling Kent beside me, I hugged him to my side as my eyes went back to the stage.

During the guitar break Bryan looked in my direction and spoke loudly in the mic, "Elly, I want you to be mine."

My hands rushed to my mouth, the box Kent had given to me forgotten for the moment on the bar. I looked to my side to celebrate my new boyfriend with Kent when I discovered that he was gone. The light pink tie he'd been wearing, probably because it was my favorite color, was beside the box he'd given me. I grabbed them both and stood on tiptoes to see if I could spot him. I saw the back of his suit as he retreated into the darkness of night. My party was dampened but not for long.

One of my co-workers came over and grabbed me, hugging me. "Bryan serenaded you! Ohmigod!" I coughed and tried to pry her arms from around my neck before they choked me.

"Thanks, MaryAnn! I'm excited too! Come, have some drinks with me!" I pulled her the short distance to the bar and we shared drinks for the next half an hour while the band finished up their set.

Bryan made his way over to me, it took a while because of all the back slaps and words of encouragement he received on his way. My friends really dug Bryan and it was obvious why. He was handsome, charming, down to earth. He was friendly and funny and he had a nerdy side. He was the complete package for me and I couldn't wait to get him alone. I smiled as I felt his arm slide around my waist and pull me back against his chest.

"Having a good birthday, Els?" I nodded and sipped my fifth

drink. "That's good. I hope when we leave I can make it the best birthday." He nibbled on my earlobe and it sent my toes curling.

He wanted to tease me? Two could play at that game. I bent over the bar, pretending to be grabbing something so that I could rub my ass against the front of his already tight jeans. I felt him shiver and heard his deep groan. I smiled with satisfaction as I turned to look at him. He shook his head at me. "You're a naughty woman."

I chuckled, "You have no idea." He nodded to the box and tie next to my drink.

"Whose is that?"

"My best friend was here. He dropped off the box and then left. I don't know where he got to. He doesn't really like crowds though. I think we might have to do a raincheck on the sexy stuff until tomorrow night." He pouted and I wrapped my arms around his neck. I pulled him down for a hot kiss. Our lips were heating up quickly but it was interrupted by yet another tap on the mic.

"Excuse me everyone but I think we all know that it's not a true party unless Elly sings us something."

I heard and felt Bryan groan as he slowly released me. I pat his chest and then made my way to the stage, cheering all the way. Bryan was right behind me and took his guitar in hand. The boys looked at me and I stared right back at them. I wasn't sure what I wanted to sing. I hadn't actually planned on singing anything. I turned the mic off briefly. "What should I sing?"

Rio tilted his head back slightly to say his piece, "Give the people what they want. Lorde."

I looked at the other two who nodded their agreement. "Okay." I flipped the mic back on and pointed at the crowd, who happened to be all of my friends. "If you know the song, I know you do, I wanna hear you sing it with me." I gave the signal to my band and then I sang Lorde's 'Royals' with a rock influence, really power-housing the chorus.

The rest of the party was me on stage, where I love being, singing to and with my friends. It was a great time but by 2am I was beat and my throat was sore. Too much screaming. I'd drunk enough water to stifle the alcohol I'd consumed earlier in the evening. As friends left I said my goodbyes and when it was mostly cleared out I started to pick things up. Bryan and Rio were behind me, tsking.

"It's your party, we can clean up for you."

I smiled at them both and I was sure they could see the gratitude on my face.

"Thank God! Have either of you seen…"

Before I could finish the question Bryan pulled the little box and the light pink tie from his jeans. How he'd gotten them in there I don't know. I sighed in relief as I took them and then hugged him. "Oh what would I do without you?"

He chuckled, "You'd be frantically trying to find your shit. Go home and get some rest. We'll take care of things. Don't worry."

Rio scoffed. "You two together? I still can't picture it. It's kind of gross. Like my brother and my sister hooking up. Fucking blech." We laughed, Bryan shook his head.

Chapter 13

"Thanks guys. I'm headed home." As I left the bar I checked my phone for text messages. There were quite a few but nothing from Kent. I sighed softly wondering if he was upset. As I rounded the corner I saw Kent's SUV parked across the street. My heels clicked as I jogged over. It was empty. I frowned and dialed Kent's number. His phone was inside and lit up.

I knew where he was. Unless he changed his hiding spot because he didn't want to see me. There was only one way to find out. I hailed the next cab I saw and gave him directions to the old abandoned tower. Within fifteen minutes I was getting out of the cab and heading up the ladder in my tight dress and heels, purse in hand. The things I did for my best friend.

I saw his outline against the sky and I walked slowly towards him. "Don't jump..." I wrapped my arms around myself because the breeze was quite nippy up there.

"That was a great party, Elly. That Bryan is a great singer. I guess congratulations are in order."

"You were at my party for all of two minutes. Are you okay?" I knelt down behind him, careful not to sit back too far lest my heels dig into my ass.

"Oh, you noticed when I left? I didn't think you would. I wanted you to have a happy birthday and it seemed like you did." He didn't sound right. I put my hand on his shoulder and gave it a gentle squeeze.

"It would've been happier if you'd have stayed with me. He's a good guy, a really good guy. We've been on a couple of dates and I was pretty sure he wanted to make it serious but I didn't know it was going to be tonight. Aren't you happy for me?" I leaned forward to try to get a look at his face.

He had a little smile and turned his face to look at me. "Yeah... Happy Birthday, Elly. I'm sorry I was being a big jerk about it."

I held the box that he'd given me on his shoulder. "I didn't open it yet. I figured you'd want to witness me opening it since seeing it happen is half the fun." I could see the tension radiating from his body but I wasn't sure why he was feeling that way or why he was suddenly acting like a jealous ex-boyfriend.

He took the box and carefully stood up, pushing me back away from the edge because he knew I was afraid of heights. "Well then, Elly," he held out the small box, "are you going to open it?"

I smiled and took the box. "I have a feeling it's not a diamond encrusted dress. The box is a little too small for that..." I glanced between him and the box.

He shook his head. "There's a story behind that gift and why I wanted to give it to you. I'm not sure it's right to give it now though under these circumstances. It is still a nice gift if I don't tell the story though." I opened the box slowly. Inside the box was a silver charm bracelet. There were already charms personalized for me and they sparkled in the moonlight. Kent shifted his eyes back towards the city as he spoke. "It's pretty so I thought you might like it, hoped you'd like it and not just pretend."

I chuckled, the thought of Jen's reaction to her birthday present seemed like so long ago now. It would forever be an inside joke between us. I reached up and put my fingers on his cheek. I pushed it to the side so he'd look at me. I could feel the tears brimming in my eyes. For more than half my life I'd wanted a gift like this from Kent and I finally had it. "I love it." I let my fingers fall from his face so I could pull out the bracelet. I held it out. "Will you put it on me? Please?"

He fumbled with the lock for a minute before it finally clasped. I turned my wrist and admired the shimmer for a minute before looking up to meet his eyes. I hugged him, the first luxurious hug in too long. He was almost divorced and I was securely attached to someone else. It was safe to hug him. I didn't have to hold back any repressed feelings or worry that the hug might spark other feelings in me. Kent was my friend and he always would be.

"I love it. I'll never take it off."

"I'm glad you like it, Elly." He broke the hug and stared down at me. It looked like he was struggling to get something out.

"I love it." I smiled and then the bombshell came.

"Elly, I love you and I've loved you for a long time. I was just too stupid to realize it."

I blinked at him, digesting what he said. He was rebounding, trying to rebound with me. I shook my head slowly and spoke softly, "Kent...you don't...I don't think...I think you're just hurting from Jen..."

"I've been waiting for a long time to do something. Something that I always wanted to do but I was too chicken shit to do it." His hand went to my cheek and he moved forward and pressed his lips against mine.

It made sense that I'd waited so long for a kiss from him that when it finally happened, Kent would do it so fast that I wouldn't see it coming. I was too stunned to react immediately but when I realized what he was doing I put my hands on his chest and pulled back.

"Kent, don't. You're very emotional right now... it's a tough time for you. I'll be here for you but I can't be here for you in that way." I watched as his face fell. He nodded in defeat.

"No...yeah, you're right. God, I'm an idiot. I'm sorry, Elly." He ran his hands through his hair, frustrated, probably with himself.

"Hey," I wrapped my arms around him and hugged him. "It's okay. Everything is going to be okay." My poor friend was hurting, most likely still crushed from the Jen cheating blow and also probably because he'd kissed me, possibly thinking it might affect our friendship and it wouldn't. I wouldn't let it. I'd let those feelings go.

"Sorry I kind of rushed out of your party. I've just had a lot of things on my mind." He wrapped his arms around me and kissed the top of my head.

"I know you do and I'm sorry I haven't been there for you like I should have been." I sighed softly and pressed my cheek against his chest. "I've been kind of a terrible friend."

"No, Elly. You've always been a great friend. You've got choices that you have to make in your life. Some that might take you away from me. Just know that I love you and always will, no matter what." I'd told him I'd loved him before, but I was pretty sure he took it in the friend way. And right now I had to do the same because even if he thought he was having deeper feelings for me he had to be wrong.

"I love you too, Kent. Always." I pulled my head back to look up at him. "Are you going to be okay?"

He rubbed a hand over his face slowly and nodded, "Yeah, I'll be fine. Don't worry about me, Elly."

"You know that's not possible." I smiled as I pinched his cheek and then stepped back to put space between us. I was maybe still a little drunk...or horny...or both. I pushed those feelings away. I had to focus.

He smiled and then nodded to the ladder. "Can I walk you home?" I nodded and he led the way.

I grinned to myself as he started down. When he was halfway I started down too. "Don't look up!"

"Don't worry. After last time I learned my lesson."

I doubted it. I grinned as I reached down and loosened my heel. I kicked it off and it went falling down, hitting him on his shoulder before falling the rest of the way to the ground. "My shoe!" The combo of my exclamation and the shoe hitting him was enough to get him to look straight up. When he realized it was just a ploy he shook his head and grumbled.

"Dammit, Elly!"

I giggled softly. "You're such a sucker."

"And you're such a tease." His feet hit the ground and he took a step back for my modesty, waiting for me to finish climbing.

"You say that like it's a bad thing." I bent down on my one shoe and grabbed the other before putting it back on. I wrapped my arm around his and walked with him in the direction of my apartment.

He looked down at my shoes and shook his head. "You're

gonna kill yourself in those things."

I looked down at my shoes and then shook my head. "Nah. They look good and they make my legs look super hot."

"Well they're not going to look sexy tomorrow when you're limping around. Climb on. And don't give me the excuse about your butt hanging out. Tie my jacket around your waist." He held out his jacket and after I took it he stepped in front of me.

"I would argue but I know you're going to pester me until I agree and I'm too tired to argue." I tied his suit jacket tightly around my waist and then jumped onto his waiting back, my arms sliding around his neck. He started walking and I smiled over his shoulder, "You're going to hurt yourself one of these days. You're getting old."

"The hell I am." He said with a grin. "You want me to run the rest of the way? Cause I will!" After saying it he jogged a few steps. I had to pee and the jostling wasn't helping.

"No!" I squeezed him hard to get him to stop jogging, my giggles disturbing the silence of the streets at 3am. "...but you are getting old." I said quickly and quietly.

"But so are you Elly, my dear." Kent smiled a little as he carried me all the way to my apartment. He walked up the walkway with me and finally put me down.

"You think I don't know that? Today is the day everyone celebrates the new wrinkles on my face." I pulled my skirt down and then untied his jacket from my waist. "Thanks for the ride. Do you want to come in?"

He didn't hesitate with his response, "It's getting kind of late, Elly. Maybe I should just walk on back and get my car. Go turn in for the night."

I wanted to say that it didn't affect me but it did, I felt the slight burn of rejection. I nodded and held out his jacket, putting a smile on for him. "Alright. Are you sure I can't call you a cab or something?" I was wishing now that I hadn't picked Bubbles because it had been within walking distance. I could see that my best friend was in distress and it was killing me that I couldn't comfort him. And I was feeling guilty that I hadn't been there to comfort him so far in his divorce process.

"Hey, I'll be fine Elly. Get some rest, alright?" He spoke softly as he brought his hand up to my cheek. "Thanks for coming to find me." He let his hand fall away from my cheek as I nodded again.

I hugged him and spoke softly into his ear, "Thanks for coming to my birthday and for the present. I love it." I pulled away and then turned away, heading for the front door to my apartment building. When I was safely inside I laid down on my bed. My mind was reeling. How could I fix this for Kent? How could I help to make him happy again? I smiled as I sat up. Brilliant. I'd set him up or go bar hopping with him. The best way to get over Jen was to throw him into a one night stand...and then he'd get the rebound sex out of the way and then he could move on to his next long-term relationship.

When I was safely tucked into bed I texted Bryan.

> ME: I'M GOING TO BED NOW.

> BRYAN: GOOD. GLAD YOU MADE IT HOME SAFELY. :-) YOU OKAY?

> ME: YES. JUST TIRED. SWEET DREAMS, BOYFRIEND. :-)

> BRYAN: YOU TOO, GIRLFRIEND. TTYL

> ME: PS KEEP YOUR HANDS WHERE GOD CAN SEE THEM TONIGHT. YOU'LL NEED TO SAVE THAT ENERGY FOR ME. MAYBE TOMORROW....;)

I plugged my phone in and turned off the light. I snuggled against my pillow as my mind raced with a sure fire plan to get Kent laid.

Chapter 14

I waited as long as I could before calling Kent. I made it to 10 am, which I thought was pretty good. He sounded groggy and I think it was in my favor that he wasn't fully awake when I bullied him into a double date with myself, Bryan and MaryAnn, my waitress friend from work.

We all three were standing outside the entrance of the mini-golf place when Kent finally showed up. I had been semi-listening to Bryan try to explain the difference between RAM and Memory as I took in MaryAnn's appearance. She looked good in a blue wrap dress that accentuated her large chest and curvy hips. Her red wavy hair was half tied back, little wisps of it played around her made up face. She was the prettiest waitress at the bar, in my opinion, and I was lucky that she was newly single and ready to mingle.

I didn't even excuse myself from my friends before running to Kent, the white platform wedges made it more difficult than usual. I wrapped my arms around him and hugged him. When he released me shortly after, I tugged at the bottom of my white dress, it barely covered my ass which had been an error of judgement on my part, especially for a game of mini-golf.

As I stepped back Bryan and MaryAnn came forward. Bryan extended his hand to Kent and shook it like they were old pals. "Didn't know Elly's friend was you, boss. Good to see you out of the shop for a change." I blinked between the two of them. His boss? Kent was

Bryan's boss? And he hadn't said anything to me? Before I could say anything about it MaryAnn slid in gracefully and offered her hand to Kent.

"Nice to meet you, Kent. Elly has told me so much about you. Please tell me you're good at mini-golf because I play to win."

Kent didn't have a chance to respond to Bryan. He smiled down at her. "I'm better than Elly at mini-golf, if that helps put your mind at ease." Kent looked at me and grinned, winking.

I pouted, "No need to advertise how much I suck."

MaryAnn smiled sweetly but her tone was a little chilly, "I had no idea you sucked, Elly." She nudged me with her elbow which sent me slightly off balance. As she wrapped her arm around Kent's I straightened myself out.

"Yeah, well..." I cleared my throat, I'd heard that MaryAnn sucked a lot but I bit my tongue and refrained, no need to ruin Kent's chance at a rebound so soon. "Let's get going or we'll miss the dinner reservations." I could see that he was not enjoying being smothered, though. I wasn't really sure how to fix that just yet without seeming like, well, like I was prying her off of him.

"You're right, Els. I was going to make a joke about balls, but I figure we'll just move on and start playing instead." Bryan grinned. It was so hot. I wasn't sure how I was going to make it through three or four hours without kissing him. PDAs in front of Kent would be weird.

"Do we want to place a bet on the game? The two with the lowest scores have to..." MaryAnn pretended to think about it but it was obvious she didn't need to. "spend seven minutes alone together somewhere before dinner?" She looked around at all of us, and ended her gaze on Kent who looked very nervous at the thought. I looked at Bryan, wondering what he would say. Would I want him kissing MaryAnn? Hell no. Would I want to get stuck maybe kissing her? Double hell no.

"What if we played guys vs girls instead? And if the girls win we get free dinner...and if the guys win...what do you guys want?" I lifted my eyebrows questioningly as we entered the building and waited briefly in line for our clubs and balls.

Kent and Bryan exchanged a look but Kent was the first to speak. "I don't know."

He chuckled as Bryan ran his hand through his hair. Bryan shrugged his shoulders. "I like the seven minutes thing, but I think it would be better with our respected others."

"But we can do that after dinner." I piped up. "If we want to bet it has to be something that can be done right after the game."

MaryAnn shrugged as we all picked out our clubs. "The winner should get something special, that's all I'm trying to get at." We made our way to the first hole but had to wait behind another foursome. I looked at Kent and smiled reassuringly trying to telepathically tell him that she couldn't rape him in public so he'd be okay. He didn't seem to get the message.

Bryan looked at Kent and Kent just shook his head, basically telling Bryan that he had to make the choice. "Hell, I don't know. It's guys versus girls. If they win then they get to ride with us to dinner, if we win..." Bryan let his voice trail off as he thought. He too was wearing a pretty tight t-shirt and those form fitting blue jeans.

I smiled up to Bryan. "Come on, babe. Use that pretty head of yours." I was refraining from smacking him on the ass, which was my first instinct. Meanwhile, MaryAnn was filling out the names on the card with the tiny pencil.

"Such wise words from Yoda here." Bryan shook his head and did smack me on my ass, causing me to jump. "Fine. The guys win then we hit the drink stand and we get a body shot before dinner."

MaryAnn looked up from the card and smiled at me and I smiled back. I wouldn't have to try to suck but I knew then that MaryAnn was going to throw the game in the favor of the guys. "Okay," we both said in unison. Bryan was up first, alphabetical order. "Hit that ball, Bryan!"

* * *

MaryAnn had officially come in last place. "Dammit! We lost, Elly!"

I grinned at Kent. "So you're going to do the body shot? I'm shocked. Can I videotape it and send it to your mom?"

Kent smirked at me and shook his head. "Only if I can record yours and send it to your mom." When MaryAnn came around to join us Kent put his arm around her shoulder. "So it looks like tequila is the shot of choice."

MaryAnn grinned and didn't touch Kent, as she'd been instructed about halfway through the game. "Sounds good to me."

I looked at Bryan, I sure as heck didn't want to see Kent cozying up to MaryAnn, even if that was the plan. "Yours too?"

Bryan nodded his head to me and he too put his arm around my shoulder just as Kent had done to MaryAnn. "Sounds really good. How about I meet you guys over there and get them set up!" Bryan didn't give time for an answer as he kissed me and moved towards the restaurant just down the road.

Internally, I was cussing like a sailor. Externally, I put on a brave, smiling face. "I'm gonna use the bathroom, I'll meet you guys there?"

MaryAnn was going to concede to whatever Kent wanted to do and waited for him to respond.

Kent shrugged his shoulders as he let his arm fall from MaryAnn's shoulders. "You sure, Elly? We can wait on you and go on then."

"No, it's fine. I'll catch up before you get there, I bet." I smiled and waved them off. MaryAnn took Kent's hand and tugged him in the direction Bryan had gone and once he was moving she let go of his hand. As they walked away I could hear her asking Kent about his store, whether he liked it. Genuinely taking an interest, or seeming to.

Chapter 15

When I got to the bar the three of them were there and MaryAnn was already stretched out on the bar top. "Body shot!" She pulled her dress up, exposing her black lace panties, her creamy white thighs, and her concave stomach. I approached, watching as Kent prepared to do his shot.

Kent's eyes moved over MaryAnn's body as she pulled her dress up. He seemed a little nervous. The bartender provided some salt and a lemon as well as the liquor. Kent lifted the lemon to let MaryAnn hold it in her mouth. He licked her stomach and applied some salt there as he poured the shot into her belly button. "Here goes," he said as he ran his tongue over the salt and slurped the alcohol out of her bellybutton and then moved up as he swallowed it to grab the lemon from her mouth with his. The young males that had gathered to get a gander at MaryAnn's hot body whooped. MaryAnn had played nice.

I stepped up and took Bryan's hand in mine, squeezing lightly. "My turn?"

MaryAnn smiled as she found my gaze. "Unless you want to do one first," MaryAnn said with a wink.

I shrugged. "Okay, what the hell." I pushed Kent out of the way and repeated the process, making a show of it. I licked slowly at MaryAnn's bellybutton, sprinkled the salt on, poured the shot and then slowly slurped, swallowed, a little falling down my chin and between my breasts and then I went for the lemon. I stood up, whoops all around. I took the lemon from my lips, held it up in the air and grinned at the boys.

Kent chuckled and shook his head. Bryan was standing amongst the guys with a grin as he watched me. We had seriously gathered the attention of the younger men there, they were starting to get closer. Bryan moved up and helped MaryAnn down from the bar and then offered his hand to me. "You ready, Sunshine?" There was something a little seductive in his eyes as he asked his question.

I smiled, "You bet." I took his hand and got up onto the bar that MaryAnn had warmed up for me. MaryAnn was standing beside Kent, watching. I was sitting up slightly, supported by my elbows, my eyes on Bryan, waiting for him to grab the hem of my dress and expose me to the many pairs of eyes watching.

Bryan smiled as he ran a hand over my leg up to the hem of the dress. There his fingers snagged it and pulled it up to show my panties and my bellybutton. He grabbed some of the salt but instead of putting it near my bellybutton he bent over, ran his tongue over my thigh right beside my panties and put it there. He took the lemon and put it into my mouth with a grin and back down he went as he put the shot in my bellybutton. He slowly ran his tongue over the salt and then moved up to my bellybutton and after he sucked it out he moved up to the lemon. He pulled it out with his teeth and dropped it beside my head on the bar. And then he pressed his lips to mine, kissing me with an untamed passion.

The kiss heated me up and despite the whooping around me I was lost in it. My hands went to his hair and I kissed him passionately in return, my back arching, trying to get my body to press against his.

There were a couple of whistles that went up when we got heated. I felt Bryan's hand reach into my hair for a moment as his tongue slid into my mouth. It seemed like there was no one else there, but soon the kiss was broken and Bryan stood beside me at the bar. "Nice shot. We'll have to do that again." He said with those perfect teeth showing in a smile.

I immediately felt the loss of him and looked up at him

longingly as I laid back on the bar, needing a moment to compose myself.

"My turn." It was MaryAnn. She smiled and took the safe route, licking the bellybutton. She salted, slurped and then took the lemon waiting in my mouth. When she was finished she pushed Kent towards me. "Your turn!"

Kent was watching, but when MaryAnn pushed him towards me he was a little stunned. "It's alright. We should get going anyway." Kent nervously moved his hand through his messy hair.

I sat up slowly, grinning at Kent. "Just give it up, MaryAnn. He's too chicken shit to do it."

Kent looked at me and tilted his head just a bit. "Chicken shit, huh?" I had no time to think before he closed the distance between us and pushed me down on the bar.

Oh shit. I didn't think he'd do it.

"Bartender, gimme a shot," he said. The bartender passed it over. Kent applied the salt to my belly and put the shot in. Just as he'd done to MaryAnn he put the lemon in my mouth with a smirk. "Ready?" he asked me, but he didn't wait for an answer.

He moved down and licked the salt from my stomach then slurped the liquid from my naval and moved up to take the lemon from my mouth. When he did so he looked down into my eyes so there was just a second pause before he stood up with the lemon in his mouth and then reached to pull it out, looking around with blushing cheeks.

I grinned and sat up behind Kent and looked at Bryan. "Did you get it?" I pulled my dress down and hopped off the bar. "He won't fire you, I promise. I won't let him."

Bryan hit the button on his cell phone and put it into his pocket. "Sure did. I sent it to you and uploaded it to my Cloud. Sorry, boss," Bryan said to him with a chuckle. "You know how she is."

Kent sighed and shook his head. "Can we go to dinner now? I'd like more than just a few shots."

I grinned. "That is so going to your mom." I held hands with Bryan, basking in the afterglow of being licked, mostly by being licked by Bryan, and led the way to dinner.

MaryAnn pat Kent gently on the back. "I didn't know they were going to record it..."

"It doesn't matter," Kent said softly. We crossed the large room to the hostess stand and followed her as she led us to a booth in the crowded restaurant.

I smiled and whispered into Bryan's ear as he moved to get into the booth. "If that kiss is any indication we are going to have one heck of a night tonight...that was...so hot..."

Bryan ran his tongue along his lips and smiled. He simply nodded his head to me. I moved in next to Bryan, practically in his lap.

The waitress stopped at our table to take our drink orders. Kent ordered a Jack and Coke with double Jack. I smiled as Bryan ordered himself a beer.

"Sweet tea, please." MaryAnn said sweetly, no longer covering her face with the menu. "And could we get an order of the bruschetta, please. And the calamari."

"I'll just have a water...and a glass of chardonnay, please. So, Kent, how was your first body shot? It looked like you enjoyed it. Certainly much more than the second one..."

"Funny funny, Elly. I can almost hear my mom now. 'Is that Elly? Kent, were you doing these things when I let you guys play video games in your room?'" He frowned and shook his head as he eyeballed me.

Bryan was grinning beside me. "I hope you're not turning this into some blackmail thing, Sunshine."

I laughed, the thought of blackmailing Kent was laughable. "There is no blackmailing. I'm not wanting anything in exchange for the movie. I'm simply going to send it along. Torturing your boss is kind of my thing." I smiled at Kent and then looked at Bryan, my smile turning angelic.

The waitress dropped our drinks off and told us that the appetisers were in and should be out shortly. Kent grabbed his drink and took a few big gulps. "That's Elly's thing. Making my life hell where my mom is concerned. She thought that I was having sex and skipping school and sneaking into Elly's house late at night. Only two out of the three were actually true."

Bryan leaned over and placed a little kiss on my lips.

MaryAnn frowned. "So which two were you doing? Sex and sneaking into Elly's house?"

I was only half listening, my lips busy with Bryan's as I kissed him back.

Kent shook his head. "Sneaking into Elly's house and skipping school." He smiled.

Bryan broke off the kiss and turned his attention to the others across the table.

"Why didn't you two ever?..." MaryAnn raised her eyebrows, looking between the two of us.

I looked across the table too, letting Kent answer that one.

Kent took a few more drinks from the cool glass in his hand. "We kissed a few times, but never sober. And I married someone else, and we see where that got me."

I rolled my eyes. "You didn't think I was hot, that's why."

Kent narrowed his eyes at me. "I was young, Elly. Besides, this isn't the time or place to talk about that." His face relaxed and he offered me a little smile.

I smiled back, though he knew I didn't mean it. "You're right. So let's talk about you...and Bryan. Why didn't you tell me he worked for you?"

Kent shrugged his shoulders. "I didn't think it mattered. Besides I found out that he was your Bryan the night he asked you out."

Bryan shrugged his shoulders. "And he never gave his friend a name so I had no idea."

"No, I know, I'm not blaming you, babe." I nodded to Bryan and then turned on Kent, "I was just shocked that you didn't mention it after you saw him at my party...when you walked me home." I hadn't exactly told Bryan that Kent had walked me home, and kissed me. And confessed to thinking he loved me. I had kind of withheld that information.

Kent shrugged his shoulders as he drank a little more of his Jack and Coke. "I knew Bryan was a good guy. It was your birthday party so I didn't feel that I needed to throw it out there that I was his boss."

MaryAnn was quiet beside Kent, taking in the dynamics.

I brought my hands up and put them both on the table and then leaned forward a bit. "Throw it out there? Don't you think you should've mentioned it, at least? 'Bryan seems like a great guy, I mean I know he is because I hired him. So feel free to bring us both free lunch someday.' Nope. Let's just put other things out there and ignore that little fact. I mean..." I glanced between Bryan and Kent, "I can only imagine the things I've said about you to him that he probably shouldn't know about his boss..."

Bryan put one of his hands on mine. "Elly, it's alright. It shouldn't be a big deal, babe."

Kent finished off the rest of his drink and pushed the empty glass forward. His cheeks were already getting rather pink from the alcohol.

MaryAnn ordered Kent another one. I looked at Bryan and nodded. "No, you're right." I shrugged softly. "It's cool that my best friend kept something from me. Lots of somethings, it seems lately."

Kent sighed as he gripped the side of his hair. Bryan took a swig of his beer. The air between me and Kent made things kind of awkward for the rest of the table.

"Sorry, I'm ruining the mood. I'll be right back." I scooted out of the booth and retreated to the bathroom. It was time for a reality check and I knew Stacy would give it to me.

> ME: AM I CRAZY?
>
> STACY: DEPENDS ON THE TIME OF THE MONTH.
>
> ME: HA HA.
>
> STACY: KENT OR BRYAN?
>
> ME: KENT. I'M GIVING HIM HELL FOR WITHHOLDING

INFORMATION. BASICALLY LYING. AM I WRONG?

STACY: NOT NECESSARILY. HOW LONG DID HE KNOW?

Shit. My birthday had only been like two days ago. I was being an asshole and irrational. About that part, at least.

ME: OKAY, I WAS WRONG. IT'S ONLY BEEN A COUPLE OF DAYS. UGH! THANKS FOR THE REALITY CHECK.

When I came back I noticed that MaryAnn and Kent were gone. I looked at Bryan with confusion. "Hey. Where did they go?"

"Back to Kent's place." He said with a click of his tongue as he took another sip of the beer in front of him. "Kent left money for dinner and told me to make sure you got something nice."

I was pissed that Kent had left the dinner. And that he couldn't wait to get away from me and be alone with MaryAnn. The emotion ran over my face but as I stared at the money it changed back to cheerful. I put my hand on his and looked at him, "Maybe we could take the rest of the money, order Chinese in and have some...fun time at your place instead?"

Chapter 16

Bryan shrugged his shoulders. "I'll do whatever you want to do, Sunshine." He smiled and took the money in his hand, leaving enough on the table for what the bill was plus a tip and pointed at a table that just sat down. "Give them the apps. On us." Bryan said with a grin and took me by the hand. "C'mon, babe. Let's get out of here."

We picked up Chinese on the way back to his place. I was my normal self again, singing loudly in the car, dancing in my seat, having forgotten completely about Kent ditching the double date. By the time we got around to cleaning up the dishes after dinner I was drunk, full, and a little lethargic and my mind was back on Kent. "Do you think Kent is fucking her right now? I mean...that was the plan.... do you think it worked?"

Bryan shrugged his shoulders as he dried a few dishes and put them away. "I don't know, babe. He seemed kind of out of it and then all of a sudden asked her to leave. Maybe he's getting his freak on, I don't know." Bryan drank another beer at dinner, but he was far from drunk.

"He probably is. I hope he's enjoying it. Do you think I should get a boob job?" I stood next to him and puffed out my chest, trying to make it look bigger.

"I think your boobs are sexy." Bryan tossed the towel over his shoulder and held his hands up like a camera. "I think they would look good on camera." Bryan grinned and whistled at me.

"I could probably get us more gigs if I had bigger boobs..."

"Elly," he said as he put his hands on my boobs to draw my

attention to him. "Your boobs are nice. They fit well in my hands and I'm sure they'd look good out in the open."

I moaned softly as I pushed his hands down to the safety of my hips. "You're trying to distract me from my tirade."

His arms moved smoothly to my lower back and pulled me against his warm, hard chest. "Perhaps I am, Sunshine. Is it working?"

"Maybe..." I giggled and pressed my chest into his. My eyes raked over him and settled on the drying towel on his shoulder. I pushed it off and watched as it fell onto the tiled floor beneath his feet.

"Tsk tsk." I glanced up in time to see him give a little shake of his head, "Getting all distracted and knocking the towel off my shoulder. That doesn't mean I'm throwing in the towel, you know."

"No, but I think it means that I am." I tilted my head back so I could look into his beautiful hazel eyes. "Are you going to take me?"

He smiled slowly, causing my insides to melt, "Right here?"

"I dunno. Can you wait until we get to your bed? Or do you have to take me right now?" I took a step backwards.

"I've waited already. What's another minute or two?" He followed me, trying to close the distance between us but I took another step, retreating towards his bedroom.

"Well in that case...what's another few days? Or weeks?" I grinned and turned on my heel. I felt his hands try to grab my waist but I escaped and headed into his room, leaving the door open for him to follow.

"Maybe we could wait another year. We'll just have to see."

I fell back onto his bed with a sigh. "Another year? I might die." I put a hand on my head for dramatic effect.

I heard him snicker and felt the bed depressing under his weight as he sat on the edge of the bed, looking over his shoulder at me.

"Me too, Els."

With his eyes on me I felt like I had to move. I kicked my heels off and stretched my arms over head.

"Mmmm, your bed is so comfy..."

"It is. You seemed to like it last time you were here too. I couldn't wake you up." He moved beside me and laid down, stretching out himself after kicking off his dress shoes.

I curled on my side facing him and tucked my hands under my cheek. "I did, I liked it a lot."

He chuckled softly, "Yeah. You were all relaxed...kind of like now."

"Mmmm..." I moaned, closing my eyes. I was drifting off and got an image of his tighty whities. "Tighty whities..." I grinned, only half awake.

"All day long." The bed moved as he turned towards me.

I reached out and stroked his cheek, I was lucky my hand landed on his cheek. "Not in the shower..." I bit my lower lip as I opened my eyes and watched my thumb glide slowly over his.

"Maybe I do. Want to see or do you want to wait here while I shower?"

I frowned softly. "I was licked by three people. Don't you think I need a shower more than you do?"

His lips turned up into a soft grin. "I guess you're right. Are you gonna walk or am I going to have to carry you?"

"I'm gonna stay here..." I ran my fingers through his hair slowly, "And you are too."

"Whatever you want, babe."

He was being so nice. Too nice. He was trying to protect me from something...or something. I crawled over him none too gently and made my way into his bathroom.

"I'll be right back." I closed the door behind me and after I did my business I started his shower. I looked at the toiletries or should I say toiletry. Just like a man. An all-in-one body and hair wash. That was it. I stripped off my clothes slowly. Should I tempt him? Yeah...

I opened the door and threw my clothes at him. He looked up in time to catch them. "Your phone is chirping a lot in there... think everything is okay?"

"Dunno!" I slammed the door. "Maybe you should look?!" I pulled the shower curtain back and got in.

After I was squeaky clean, I toweled off my hair with the hand towel and then went back into the bedroom to check on Bryan. He was sitting on the bed and I closed the distance between us. He had my phone in his hand and I smiled at him as I straddled his lap. "Who was it?" I pressed my lips to his neck, which tasted salty.

"Kent."

I tried to keep Kent's face from my mind, I didn't want him to kill my sexual buzz with Bryan.

"Oh?" I licked my way up to his ear and suckled on it softly.

"He said he's sorry for kissing you the other night."

I froze and pulled back to look at his face. His calm voice was deceiving how he truly felt. I could see in his eyes that was in pain.

"It was a mistake and he's sorry. Said he wants lunch or dinner this week because he needs some Elly-time."

"Oh..." I stared at my phone for a moment, shaking my head. "Bryan I...I was going to tell you."

"Mmmhmm..." he said softly as he twirled the phone in his hand. "Maybe you should text him back and give him your answer." He held the phone out to me.

"No. He can wait. I'm here with you. I want to be here with you." I looked up to make sure he could see the sincerity in my eyes. "He kissed me and I pulled away."

He set the phone on the bed next to his thigh. The flesh of his cheek pulsed as he clenched his teeth. "I believe you."

I ran my fingers over his tense jaw, his neck and back into his hair. "I'm sorry I didn't tell you..."

"I'm glad it came out now. I'm not sure how I would've reacted if it had come out later."

I pressed my lips to his hard, trying to distract him from my error in judgement. He didn't pull away which was a good sign. I laced my fingers into his hair and then pulled tight while kissing him. I moaned, my body already excited at the thought of a mild dose of makeup sex.

I felt his hands at my hips and I wiggled on top of him in response. I felt the cool air on my breasts as the towel came loose and fell around my hips. He pressed into the kiss as one of his hands came up and seized my breast. I arched my back, pressing it further into his hand and rolled my hips against his jeans. His other hand grabbed the towel and threw it onto the floor. If I'd been without my lips against his I would've said something about throwing in the towel. As it was his hand was on my bare ass, squeezing it with every lift of my hips, the feel of his rough, warm hand made me wet.

I was getting impatient so I pulled away and grabbed his shirt, pulling it up and over his head. "I want to feel your skin against mine. All of it," he murmured as his hands reached between us as he unbuttoned his jeans. I left his lap and moved behind him.

I pressed myself against his rounded back and ran my hands over his bare chest. "You're so warm...so sexy..." I whispered, softly.

He pushed his clothes off onto the floor and then sat back up. I nibbled on his ear as my arms snaked around his chest. I released him and laid back onto the bed and he followed me. He placed himself between my legs on his knees and grabbed my ankle. From there he kissed up to my knee and then his tongue left a wet little trail the rest of the way up to my hot, wet center.

I gasped, "Bryan..." I grabbed his hair when he got close enough and tugged, it didn't stop his tongue from licking my slit. I groaned as he lapped at my clit and lifted my hips in response. He started further up my body, his lips left soft kisses along the skin of my stomach until his nose nuzzled against one of my breasts. "Oh god... feels so good... you're making me so wet..."

As he took one of my nipples in his mouth he pressed his erection against my inner thigh. "I hope you're off work tomorrow..." he whispered softly. The cool air rushed over the wet nipple that slipped from his mouth and I moaned, my fingers still tight in his hair.

"I want..." my voice was drowned out by the chirping on my phone. My breath hitched as he moved to my other nipple, taking it into his hot mouth. "Bryan...wait..." I pulled him back as I sat up, my breath coming in short pants because I was so turned on.

He looked me over, his eyes smoking with lust. "Why? What's wrong?" I bit my lower lip and shook my head.

"I'm not ready." I knew that if I gave into him, if I let him have me the mystery would be gone. He'd bolt, or cheat or start to distance himself. It happened every time. Sex complicated things.

He was staring at me, searching my face for a better reason than that. He exhaled deeply and nodded as he climbed off the bed and went into the bathroom. He shut the door behind him and I heard the shower turn on.

"Shit..." I muttered to myself. I grabbed my phone and turned it over. Kent again...

Chapter 17

Before I could even get a word out after answering my phone, I heard Kent's voice. "Don't hang up, I'm sorry I'm interrupting you...just...just listen. Okay?" Again he didn't seem to wait on me to acknowledge it. "MaryAnn and I kissed. We touched each other and we fooled around, but I couldn't have sex with her. I'm sorry. I wanted to tell you. It didn't feel right...I closed my eyes and imagined you and it felt wrong to pretend she was you... so I didn't. I don't want a rebound because it's not going to change the way things are."

I sighed and spoke softly, "Kent. You don't know that. You can't know that."

"Of course I know that. I don't want to have sex with someone else. I don't want someone else. I'm sorry. I appreciate you trying to be a true friend, but," he sighed on the other end of the phone.

"But nothing. What are you saying? You're going to be celibate for the rest of your life because you can't fuck me?" My voice raised slightly as my anger increased. He was being ridiculous.

"Elly, it's not about the sex. I screwed up. I know this is probably going to fuck up our friendship, but, I love you. I always have, I always will, and when you finally see it, I hope that one day we can be together."

"Oh God, Kent. You're just," it was my turn to sigh again. "We can't be together that way," I spoke gently trying to break it to him easily.

"I wanted to tell you how I felt. I wanted to let you know that I didn't fuck Mary Ann, which I'm sure she'll tell you all about, and I wanted to say to you that I'm sorry. I'm sorry I made the wrong choice so many years ago when it was always staring me in the face and drinking Mountain Dew with me."

I soaked in his words and yet a part of me was still not convinced he meant it. "That was a long time ago. You didn't want me then, why now? Why...Now?"

The phone on his side was silent for a moment. "Jen wanted me, and I had no idea how to handle it. I'm sorry I pulled you along on all those dates as a third wheel. I'm sorry I didn't just tell Jen to fuck off. I'm sorry that you weren't my only choice for Prom. I was a teenager who didn't want to hurt anyone, but I hurt my best friend because I was stupid."

"I..." I stuttered and then sighed. "And I was pining and drooling over you. I ...I let that go. You'll have to learn how to do the same. What can I do to help? Block your calls? Be a total bitch to you?"

"You do whatever you feel is right, Elly. I couldn't live with myself anymore without you knowing how I felt."

The shower turned off and I got up wrapping a blanket around myself, tucking it in at my chest as I made my way to the living room. "Isn't that convenient for you to lay this all on me. I held it all in for all those years. But this isn't about me. It's about you."

"No, Elly. It's about us."

"Kent there is no 'us' outside of our friendship." I started pacing the living room.

"Meet me and look me in the eye and tell me that. Then maybe I'll believe you and leave you alone."

I scoffed. "That's such bullshit." When he didn't say anything for a few long seconds I sighed and caved in. I'd do almost anything to get him to shut up about the fantasy he'd created for us. "Fine. When?"

"One hour, the park."

"What?! Kent, it's after midnight. How about tomorrow morning at the park? Like nine-ish."

"How about one hour and this'll all be over, one way or another." He sounded like he wasn't going to back down. The door to the bathroom opened and Bryan came out with a towel wrapped around his waist as his hands shook through his damp hair.

"I'm a little...busy."

"So am I. I'm busy leaving to go to the park." Kent hung up the phone on his side.

"Goddammit." I stared at the Call Ended on my phone and then went back into the bedroom to collect my clothes, get dressed, and confront Bryan. I looked him over and admired his bare chest. "Hey...So I have some bad news..."

Bryan was running a brush through his hair when I came back into the bedroom. He watched me for a few moments as I dressed and smiled when I approached him. "Bad news? What's goin' on?"

"Kent needs to talk."

Bryan chewed on the inside of his lip. "I'm guessing right now, huh?"

"Apparently. I'm really sorry," I hugged him.

I could feel the apprehension on his end of the hug. "You want me to give you a ride?"

"No I'll be okay."

"Well, call me if you need me. Send me a text when you figure out what's up and if you're heading home or coming back this way." He leaned his head in and gave me a soft kiss on the lips.

I moaned and whined against his lips. "I don't wanna go. I wanna stay here with you."

"Hey, I'll still be here if you want to come back, minus a towel."

"Mmm. Don't tempt me." I smiled and all but ran away before my willpower to do so failed me.

* * *

As I approached the park I searched for Kent. After a moment of searching, I found him sitting on the hood of his SUV, his hands pushed into the front pockets of his pants.

I inched forward slowly, wrapping my arms around myself. I looked up into his eyes. "Kent..."

Kent turned his gaze towards me. I'd looked into those dark eyes so many times before. What was different about them now? He sat there and stared back at me, waiting for me to speak the words he'd dared me speak to him. "There is no us outside of our friendship." I shrugged my shoulders and looked down. "Satisfied?"

I watched the muscles of his jaw tighten. "Fair enough. Thanks, Elly. I needed that." The words came from him softly as he slid from the hood of the car and moved towards the car door.

"Where are you going?"

"I don't know."

"Kent..."

He opened the door to the car and then paused and looked at me. I followed him and grabbed the door so he couldn't speed away without hurting me. "You need to get out of the rut that is your high school life..."

"Actually, you put me right back where I was, because now I know how you felt. I'm sorry I made you feel this way, Elly."

"I'm over it."

"I'm still not, so you'll have to forgive me if I don't handle the rejection so well."

"I'm not... I'm not rejecting you. I am with someone."

"You rejected me when you came out here to meet me and tell me we'd never be anything but friends." He turned away from the car, shoved his hands back into his pockets and started walking away.

"Kent! Come on! Quit being such a baby..." I called to his retreating back.

Kent just shook his head and waved his hand in the air as he continued to walk.

"Kenny!" I frowned at his back and slammed the door of his car. It had no effect. His feet were carrying him a little ways into the park, where he sat down on a bench. I blew out a hot breath and looked around. My eyes caught on the flowers laying hopeful in the front seat and I wish they hadn't. What was he doing with the flowers if he thought I was going to come out here and tell him there was nothing between us? My gut twisted as I walked towards the bench he'd perched on. "What do you want me to do? Break things off with Bryan and date you?"

"Because I'm selfish, yes. I know it isn't fair, Elly. I'm sorry I even tried to call you tonight. I probably interrupted a good night for you guys."

"That is selfish. If I had told you to dump Jen and date me instead, would you have?"

Kent shook his head slowly, his eyes on his hands in his lap. "I would love to say yes, but I'm not that kind of guy, and I know you're not that kind of girl."

"But you have the balls to demand that of me now? A little hypocritical don't you think?"

"Entirely. That's why I was walking away. You shouldn't have to screw up a potential—" His eyes closed as he sighed, "a potentially wonderful relationship all because I asked you to."

"It pains you to say that?" I looked at him with wide eyes.

"It pains me to see my chances slipping away. I wish you could be happy with me, but I just want you to be happy even if it's not with me."

"Good. Then stop this crazy talk."

"Sorry, Elly. It's out in the open and I can't take it back. I won't."

I glanced at my phone after it chirped in my hand. It was Bryan.

BRYAN: YOU ALRIGHT, BABE? KENT'S NOT GOING ALL WEIRD ON YOU, RIGHT?

Kent watched me as I looked at my phone and his eyes shifted away. "Why don't you go back to, Bryan? It's late and he's probably worried about you."

ME: YES. HE'S BEING WEIRD.

I typed as I talked. "He wants to know if you're being weird."

BRYAN: DO I NEED TO COME KICK HIS ASS?

Kent shook his head again. "Now he's probably asking for a fight or something. Maybe to be your hero?" The muscles in his jaw tightened and then loosened. "Just go on, Elly."

"Don't tell me what to do. How did you know he wanted to

kick your ass?" I typed my response quickly.

ME: REALLY? YOU'D COME KICK HIS ASS?

"It's a typical guy response when their girlfriend is threatened or ogled. Protect the thing that makes children. It's in our DNA."

BRYAN: I DON'T GIVE A DAMN IF HE'S MY BOSS. I'M GETTING IN THE CAR.

ME: BRYAN, IT'S FINE. KENT IS GIVING ME A RIDE HOME.

BRYAN: HE'D BETTER NOT TRY TO FUCKING KISS YOU AGAIN.

I looked at Kent. "Drive me home?"

He shrugged his shoulders. "If you want me to." Kent seemed to be defeated at this point. He'd move past it. He did when he was going through the stuff with Jen.

I sighed. "Please?"

"Right. C'mon then." The words came from him softly as he stood from the bench and started to walk back to his car. He unlocked the passenger side first. "The flowers are yours." He climbed in behind the wheel and started the car.

I picked up the flowers and put them on my lap. "What's next for you?"

"I don't know, Elly." He said as drove me to my apartment. I nibbled on my lower lip as I stared at him in the darkened car. How could I get him past this without pushing another girl at him?

"Kent, you're depressing me." I looked from the flowers to his face and then back again. I could feel the tension in the car, so thick you could cut it with a knife.

"Don't let me get you down." He glanced at me and I could tell he was forcing the smile he had trained on me. I sighed heavily as I put my head back against my headrest.

"This is stupid. Pull over." He glanced at me, a worried look on his face.

"What? Why do you want me to pull over?" I grabbed the steering wheel and tried to force him over. He gripped the wheel tighter. "Alright!"

I let my hands slip off the wheel as he put his foot on the brake and pulled onto the side of the road. He wouldn't meet my eyes after he put the car in park. I unbuckled my seatbelt, threw the flowers in the back and then straddled him. My hands slid through his dark, messy hair and my head came closer to his as my eyes looked over his face. He looked unsure, confused.

"What are you waiting for?" I whispered as I stared at him, only our breaths between us.

"Is this some kind of game? I'm not really in the mood to play if it is..." Here I was throwing myself at him, giving him access to prove how much he wants me and he rejects me... Again.

"Right..." I hung my head and moved to fall back into my seat but his hands clamped onto my waist, holding me firmly in place. I glanced up and saw his Adam's apple bob before pulling my gaze up to his beautiful brown eyes. I chewed on my lower lip softly. What the hell was I doing? I was with Bryan. I'd been with him for like two days! I needed to give him a shot, a fair shot. My chest heaved as I started to panic. He must have seen it in my face because he let his grip on my waist go.

"Elly, this isn't..."

I nodded and slid back into my seat beside him.

"No, you're right. It's not right. If we do this then it has to be when we're both single and available." Kent swallowed hard again and then nodded, his hands seemed to be moving in slow motion as they gripped the steering wheel again. He put the car in gear, and within minutes we were stopped again in front of my apartment.

Chapter 18

I showed up at Bryan's house the following evening. I'd been thinking about the situation with Kent all day, and decided that what I said was true; I wanted to see how things with Bryan played out. I'd built Kent up for so long that I wasn't sure if he was reality or fantasy. But Bryan, he was reality and I wanted to give our relationship a fighting chance.

I didn't tell him I was coming over, but rather showed up just after dinnertime. I knocked on the door and waited, my teeth gently clamping down on my lower lip. I wasn't looking forward to the chat I felt we had to have.

The door opened and Bryan stood there in a pair of tight blue jeans and a white v-neck t-shirt. When his eyes moved onto me he grinned. "Hey, babe. If I knew you were coming over I'd have made more food."

"That's okay." I tried to peek around him to see if he had company and then back at him. "Am I interrupting anything?"

Bryan shook his head. "No, I was just putting leftovers away. It's just me. Want to come in?" He asked as he moved to the side so I could come in. "It'll just be a few minutes while I finish up. Want a drink or something while you wait on my slow ass?" He grinned.

I returned the grin and shook my head. "No, I'm okay. Thanks. I'll just wait on the couch until you're done; if that's alright..."

"That's fine. I'll join you in a minute." He pulled me into his arms for a hug and pressed a soft kiss to my lips.

I smiled after pulling back from the brief kiss and, when he turned away, I smacked his ass. "I'll miss you."

He skipped from the smack and turned his head with a grin. "I know, sweetheart." He offered me a wink and moved on to the kitchen.

I chuckled to myself as I got comfy on the couch. I removed my shoes and pulled my long, black peasant skirt up over my ankles. As I waited for him, my mind drifted back to Kent. I wondered what he was going to do now that I'd turned him down. Was he going to try to reconcile things with Jen? Was he going to go find another woman? Would he indeed remain celibate? He'd probably throw himself into his work and stay inside playing video games all day. Whatever he did, it wasn't my problem. He was my friend but nothing more, I needed to let his own mother worry about him.

My mind shifted back to Bryan. He was the right choice. He was the sensible choice. And he adored me. And I adored him.

I heard Bryan in the kitchen. He was whistling the song he'd sang to me that night at my birthday party. I heard dishes moving around and then the fridge open. After a few minutes, Bryan vaulted over the back of the couch and put his arm around my shoulders. "I'm here, gorgeous."

"That's good, I was starting to wonder if you'd been eaten by a bear or something."

"No, no bear. Not eaten at all. Is there something eating you, though?"

I cleared my throat and sat up straight. I turned my body towards him and looked down for a moment to collect my thoughts. What was I going to say? I'd worked it all out in my mind on my way over. "Bryan, about last night..."

Bryan removed his arm and put his hand on my knee. "Did you sleep with him?" He asked with a soft voice. "Because if you didn't, then whatever happened doesn't matter."

I frowned at him. "So if I told him I loved him it wouldn't matter to you so long as I didn't sleep with him?"

"All I did last night was wonder what the two of you were talking about that was so important. I wondered if he told you how much he loved you, and I wondered if you told him the same. I wondered until I started to worry. I got jealous..." he turned his eyes away from me. "Then I realized that I would find out one way or another. You'd either break up with me, or you wouldn't. In that moment I decided I would trust you to do what's right." His eyes shifted back up to mine.

I exhaled loudly and shook my head, looking down, "I don't know why I'm angry at you. I didn't sleep with him. But he does think for some god forsaken reason that he's in love with me, which is just ridiculous."

"I don't dislike the guy. But isn't he like fifteen years too late on telling you that? I don't know you like he does, but I can't see how he passed you up. I don't know the story."

"Like... Nine, at least." I nodded and then shrugged my shoulders. "He..." I closed my eyes and shook my head. "It doesn't matter. The fact is," I reached out and grabbed his hand, pulling it to my lips. I kissed it and smiled up to him, "I want to be with you. I definitely picked you, hands down."

"Good." Bryan grinned as he quickly finished up his beer. "I got to brush my teeth and then we can get some sleep."

I had brushed mine before I came over so I felt confident in going straight to bed. I went to his drawers and opened them up to find a T-shirt to sleep in, as he disappeared into the bathroom.

I heard the trashcan thud from the bottle and heard the water turn on as he brushed his teeth. After a few minutes he came out to join me. He undid his pants and pushed the jeans down, kicking them into the hamper, his shirt following closely.

My clothes were neatly folded on top of his dresser next to his camera and I was already under the covers in his T-shirt and my panties. "Hurry up, man. It's cold!"

"Patience, woman." He crawled into the bed under the covers with me. Bryan turned, switching the lamp off.

I clung to him like a second skin, wrapping my body around his. He was like a furnace, except for the places my cold skin would leech the heat from him. "You are cold!"

"I told you." I snuggled up with him. "Mmm..." I closed my eyes, my cheek and hand on his chest.

Bryan kept his eyes on the ceiling. "Where's my goodnight kiss?"

I slowly pushed myself off his chest and inched up until my lips found his and pressed against them softly. I felt him press forward a little more.

I broke the kiss and placed another quick one on his lips before pulling back so I could roll over and get some sleep.

"Goodnight, Elly." He said softly. He rolled over and put his arm around my waist.

"'Night, Bryan." I whispered softly.

He placed a little kiss on my shoulder. "I'll see you in the morning. It's your turn for breakfast, I think."

"Hope you like beer for breakfast." I murmured.

I heard him chuckle but he didn't say anything else.

"...How do you like your sex?"

"Hard."

I swallowed hard, I shouldn't have asked. "Oh, okay..."

"Hard, fast... Until there's no energy left." His voice a soft whisper.

"And that takes like... Five minutes?"

"Sometimes a little longer, but considering how long it's been for me... Yeah, probably five minutes..."

I smiled, "Doesn't hurt you male ego to admit that?"

"Hell no. I know I can last. It's just when it's been a while that—yeah—it happens."

"That's the only time it happens?"

"No. If I get too excited I can't last for shit. I can't believe I'm sharing this. I'm supposed to be the best lay ever."

"According to who?" I put my hand over his arm that was around my waist.

"That's what my ego says. I've had nothing but compliments."

"I'm so bad I don't get acknowledged at all." I bit my lip, not believing I'd told him that either. Being in the dark always made me feel like I could divulge secrets. Luckily for me, I wasn't often with anyone alone in the dark.

"I find that hard to believe, Elly. I've seen the way your body moves when you dance. I can see the emotion in the movement. I think you'd be killer in the sack."

"It's been awhile for me too. A long while. But I'm telling you, I'm a terrible lay." I shrugged one shoulder a bit.

"I just can't agree with you. If you believe that, then show me."

"No, I want to enjoy having you as a boyfriend for a bit longer."

Bryan chuckled. "Fair enough. But I'm not gonna believe you."

"Don't hype me up, you'll definitely be disappointed then."

"Whatever, Elly." He placed a soft kiss on my shoulder. I moaned softly.

His warm lips moved over and placed another soft kiss beside it.

Another moan escaped as me pushed my hips back, my ass pressing against him.

I felt his arm tighten around my waist a little. The soft kiss on my shoulder moved to a bare spot that his shirt didn't cover.

I bit my lower lip and sucked in a gasp, rocking against him slowly.

Bryan's teeth grazed where his lips had touched. "I want you so bad. But..." there was a little growl. "I don't want you to feel pressured."

"You want to talk about it?" I reached back, holding tight on the back of his neck to keep his face at my neck.

He nibbled on my neck, then ran his tongue over it. The arm that had tightened around me now lifted a little so his hand could slide under his shirt as it brushed by the line of my panties and moved up over my stomach.

My back arched, my plump ass rubbing against the front of his boxer briefs again. My butt slid away as his hand moved up my stomach. I sucked it in tight, letting his hand explore, leaving my skin covered in goosebumps. "Before we get too excited... Do you have a condom?"

His hand retreated as he turned away from me for a moment to open the drawer by the bed. I heard a crinkle sound and the drawer shut. The hand with the condom put it in front of me so I could see it as he let his hand slide back under my shirt and explore the curves of my skin, eventually ending up at my breast.

My hand reached behind and between us, slowly rubbing him through the stretchy fabric. My breasts were a little less than a handful but my nipples were very receptive. As soon as he touched them they shriveled up and turned into hard nubs. He touched them both in turn until they were hard, then placed kisses down my neck to the collar of the shirt. His hand left my breasts and I held the whimper in my throat as they moved slowly down my stomach. I thrust my hips forward, eager for his hand to be inside my panties, touching me again like he had in his car. My hand squeezed him, stroking slowly.

Bryan's hand slid down under the line of my panties and down between my thighs. I felt his fingers rub against my lower lips as his hips slowly started move with my hand.

I moaned softly and threw my leg back over his, spreading myself open for him. "Please..." I felt one of his fingers slide inside of me.

"You're so wet for me," he whispered right into my ear. His finger withdrew and moved up, reaching for the condom on the bed in front of me. With one hand he tore it open and leaned back. Before too long the condom covered his dick and it was pressed against my slit.

I shuddered, my hand on the back of his neck again. I tilted my hips so he could more easily penetrate me but just before the thrust there was a loud knocking on the front door and then the doorbell rang several times in a row.

He groaned loudly, still waiting at my entrance. "It's the guys. I know it."

"Why the hell would it be the guys?" I reached back and put my hand on his ass, pushing him forward, "Just ignore it!"

Bryan sank into me just a little and moaned into my ear. "So... Tight."

James banged on the door and yelled through it, "I know

you're in there, dammit! I'm hungry!! Let me in!"

I heard his head hit the pillow behind me.

"Bryan, just ignore him." I hissed, smacking his ass.

There was silence.

Bryan let his hips start to move again until he pressed all the way into me. God, he was big too. His cock throbbed inside of me as he nipped at the skin of my neck. "God, I want to fuck you."

I moaned and whimpered as he entered me. My eyes were closed against the outside world. "Yes...please...fuck me."

There was some male giggling outside Bryan's bedroom window. James stood outside, a phone in front of his face, pointed right at us.

He pulled out of me up to the tip and paused.

"James, what the hell are you..." Rio's face showed a moment later, "Holy hell!! Not cool man!" Rio tried to grab for the phone but James was too quick and went dashing away.

"Kill...him...I'm going to kill him." Bryan said through gritted teeth. Luckily we were covered up, but it was still bad enough.

I opened my eyes wide and gasped, thankful for the sheets that covered us. "Oh god!" I rolled off the bed and ran to the dresser, pulling on my skirt. "I'm going to kill him first!"

Bryan's phone pinged with an incoming message.

I was out the door before I saw it, walking with purpose down the hallway. "JAMES!!"

There was more pounding on the door and James called through, "I'm here Elly-baby! Open up for Daddy!"

I got to the door and flung it open. James saw Bryan coming and grabbed me, shielding himself with me before I could protest. "I deleted it, man! It's gone, don't hurt me!!"

Rio came in and got between James and Bryan, putting his forearm on Bryan's chest to hold him back. "Woah, woah."

Rio's girlfriend, Stacy, was standing back, watching. Two six-packs in her hands. I tried to turn around but James held me tightly in place, his hands on my hips.

"A call would have been fucking nice!" Bryan said towards

James. "Much less the shit at the window!"

"Dude, you said to come by anytime! How was I supposed to know a fucking RSVP was a must? I didn't know this was Queen Fucking Elizabeth's castle!"

Bryan pushed against Rio, and James was lucky Rio was a big enough guy to hold Bryan back from kicking his ass.

I was pissed but I looked down, biting my lower lip to keep from laughing. James felt my ribs moving and looked around my shoulder and then pointed at my face. "See. Elly's a honey badger, dude. She doesn't give a fuck."

I tried to move out of James' grasp but it was pointless, I put my serious face back on. "No, I do give a fuck. That was so not cool. You're just so stupid sometimes, I have to laugh."

"You were just going to ignore us while you got your rocks off!" James accused.

"Yeah... I was. When was the last time you were laid?"

James paused as he counted in his head, "52 hours..."

"Right. It's been fucking years for me. So back the fuck off." James released me with a gasp, his hand over his mouth in disbelief.

"Elly..." James was trying to say something but he couldn't seem to get it out.

Bryan was standing there, hands still clenched in fists. "Happy now, fucktard?"

Rio grinned, probably happy that his adopted sister had been sex-sober for so long.

James looked at Bryan and pointed to his own shocked face. "Do I look happy, bro?! This is a crime!!"

I rolled my eyes.

"Just..." Bryan sighed. "Just get the fuck in here and shut the damn door. There's fucking leftovers in the fridge."

Stacy, no longer afraid of getting accidentally punched, walked in and went to the kitchen to put the beer in the fridge.

James grabbed my hand and dropped to his knees, looking up at me, "Elly, you can use me anytime, anytime. I swear, I'll use protection, I'll be gentle or do you like a whore, whatever you like."

I blinked as Rio grabbed James by the back of his shirt and pulled him up. "Alright, lover boy, that's enough. Leave her alone before you get your ass kicked by her boyfriend." Rio turned to Bryan, "You are her boyfriend, right?"

Bryan nodded his head. "Yes, and about five seconds away from kicking his ass if you don't get that asshole stuffing his fucking face, Rio, so he shuts the hell up."

Rio pushed James towards the kitchen, patting him on the back, leaving the two of us alone.

I looked at Bryan, my cheeks still slightly flushed from his intrusion on my body. "Well..."

"Maybe there should have been some rules there, Elly..." he said softly, his anger slowly fading. "I'm sorry... I'm just so angry with him, but..." His eyes met with mine as his tongue ran over his lips. "I..." I could see the lust plainly in his eyes.

"You want to fuck me in the bathroom real quick?" I raised my eyebrows questioningly as James came back into the living room, a huge helping of leftovers on a plate.

"This shit is good, man. You cook this, Elly?"

I turned to James. "Um, no. I don't cook."

James looked heartbroken, "Damn..."

I felt Bryan come up behind me and press himself against my backside, his cock growing quickly to full arousal. "That was me, you jackass. That was supposed to be my lunch tomorrow, so I think you owe us dinner on you." After his words I felt the slight tickle or air against my ear. "I'll be waiting for you. I want to shove my cock so far inside of you you're going to feel it when you wake up." Bryan stepped away after his hand slapped my ass and he moved towards his room.

I jumped and James looked at me funny when the blush colored my cheeks from his sexy talk. "What the hell was that?"

I shrugged, "I don't know. He was projecting his anger onto me, I guess. Thanks for that. I gotta get a bra on."

"Not on my account!"

"I do, for Stacy's sake," I said. James nodded, accepting that answer. When I passed by him I slapped him hard on the ass. "Behave yourself. Enjoy the hot tub out back. Save a spot for me, 'kay?"

"Will do, Els. Hey guys, hot tub time!!!" James took off towards the kitchen and I went into Bryan's bathroom and locked the door as I pressed my backside against it.

Bryan was leaned against the sink, naked once more, and he was ready to go. Those lust-filled eyes looked over my body as he held a new condom in his hand.

I was panting softly, partly for the brief run, partly from my excitement. I stripped off his t-shirt and then pulled down my skirt and panties in one swoop. "We have to be quick or James will come sniffing around here again." I approached him quickly, putting my arms around him, kissing him passionately. It was apparently too good for him. He had finished and so quick. His head lifted when I started to kiss my way up his neck and when my lips found his, he returned the kiss.

"Thanks for cleaning out the cobwebs," I whispered.

"I..." his words seemed to be stuck inside as his eyes opened. He chuckled. "You're welcome."

I kissed him again, gently, lovingly.

He returned the kiss just as I did and ended with his forehead pressing to mine. "We better join the others before there's another issue."

I nodded, eyes on his. "We need to disjoin first..."

Bryan bit his lip and returned me to the sink. "Sorry...I wanted to stay like that a little longer."

"I think the condom is making me...hurt."

"I was a little rough," he almost whispered as he pulled out of me, his hand pulling the condom from his dick.

I grabbed his wrist and held it up, frowning at the condom. "Shouldn't there be more stuff in there?"

He examined it, "Shit. It broke." I let go of his wrist and suddenly I felt a little dizzy.

He let the condom fall in the trash can where it landed with a wet thunk. "I'm—I'm sorry, Elly."

I shook my head, my eyes staring off as I looked to the door. "I need a minute to clean up..."

He nodded and quickly left the room. I heard him yelling, "James, you son of a bitch!" and that was the beginning of what turned out to be a super fun night.

Chapter 19

"Hey, Elly." My body stiffened as I heard a voice behind me. I knew exactly who it was and I was not eager to see him. Not after what had happened between us. And especially not standing in line at the pharmacy waiting to pick up my morning after pill.

I turned around, and looked up into Kent's eyes, "Kent. Hey. What are you doing here?"

"Picking up medication," he said, "What are you doing here? The same I suppose?" He chuckled just a little.

I smiled and shrugged, "Um yep..." I was next in line but I motioned for him to go first. Maybe I could get rid of him and save both of us some embarrassment. "Go ahead I'm sure you've got places to be."

"Not really. Bryan's got the shop so I decided to go out for a while." He shook his head and let me stay where I was.

I nodded with a curt smile. "Right. Ok." I turned back around and stepped up to the counter. I spoke real low so Kent wouldn't overhear.

The pharmacist was not so subtle, "Did you want the brand name morning after pill or the generic one? The cost difference is $40."

I answered quickly, "Generic is fine."

I showed my ID, paid with cash and was handed the pill in a little white paper bag. I turned back around and smiled at Kent. "Your turn. I'll see ya..."

"Uh..." Kent nodded his head, he looked a bit surprised. "Yeah. It was good to see you as always, Elly." The words came out softly, underlined with hurt, but he moved up in line to pick up his medicine. It was some sort of sinus medication.

I was almost out of the store when I realized that I'd forgotten to get water to flush the pill down with. I purchased it and as I was on my way towards the door I bumped into Kent. "Oh, sorry. You can go first..."

Once again he shook his head. "No, go ahead."

"No, really, go ahead." I waited.

Kent shook his head. "I insist, Elly. Go on."

"Ok. Thanks." I ducked my head and walked in front of him.

I stopped at the side of the building to open my water and take my pill. The sooner the better for those little guys. Kent watched me take the pill as he walked by. He wanted to stop to talk to me, that much was obvious. Once he was in his car I waited to see him look my way and then I waved at him. He returned the wave and then seemed to fight with himself as he rolled down the window.

"Lunch? On me? Don't worry, just friends."

I considered it. I hadn't had breakfast since I rushed out of Bryan's place without waking anyone. And I didn't have time to go to the market before my work shift. Kent wasn't trying to seduce me with dinner, and even if he were he knew that I was having sex with Bryan now. It should be completely harmless.

I nodded, "Okay."

"C'mon then. We can go someplace close to the shop so you can go see Bryan if you want. After, I'm gonna go home. Or we can get a bite close to your house."

"Sure. Whatever works for you. I'm getting a free ride." I got into his car and buckled up. I put my purse and water between my legs.

When he worked he always wore nice polo shirts and khaki pants. He looked very presentable. "Bryan could probably use some company at the shop. We can go to the sub shop or the Greek restaurant close by my house. Your choice."

"Greek, I guess. I don't really want to bother him at work..."

"I was," Kent sighed, "just saying there's not much going on and if you want to go by and see him, you can. If you don't want to, then I'll just take you someplace close to your house."

"I just don't want to distract him, that's all. And I'll see him later."

There was a nod of his head. "Then Italian, Pizza, or Japanese since those are nearby your house?"

I glanced at Kent, taking him in. "Japanese, I guess."

"Alright." Kent drove. The air between us was awkward because of the other night. "How's the band doing?" he finally asked.

"Good. We had quite a night last night... James, our bassist, he almost got his ass kicked like ten times. He's such a flirt. It tends to get him into trouble."

Kent chuckled, "Sounds like a hell of a party."

"We played Name That Tune and Strip Poker. It was fun." I stared straight ahead.

"I'm glad you're having fun, Elly." Kent pulled into the parking lot of the restaurant.

I glanced at him. "I always have fun."

Kent nodded his head as he unbuckled his seatbelt. "I remember. It's one of the reasons I hung out with you all the time." He turned his head and stuck his tongue out at me before he got out of the car. I followed. He held the door for me to go in in front of him. It was a seat yourself restaurant, so he grabbed a few menus as we went by the stand. I seated us near the back.

"I haven't been here before. Have you?" I asked.

There was a nod of his head. "Their vegetable stir fry is actually really good, and the hibachi chicken. Those are the only things I tend to eat here."

"Do you eat out a lot?" I picked up the menu and looked it over briefly.

"Yeah. I hardly ever eat at home and just snack at work." Kent never picked up the menu, apparently he already knew what he wanted to eat.

"What are you going to get?"

"The vegetable stir-fry with white rice."

I tucked my legs under the seat. "That's what I was going to get. Should I get the chicken instead?"

"How about you get the vegetable stir-fry and I'll get the chicken and you can try a bite or two to see if you like it. Deal?"

"Ok." His eyes looked down to his menu on the table. "Are we still friends, Elly?"

"Are we still friends? Yeah, I guess so. Nothing has changed really." I glanced at him, pretending we were cool. His eyes were still looking down at the table.

"Will the awkwardness go away? I'm afraid to try and call you. Afraid to give you a hug. I don't want to," he paused, "be in the way."

"Welcome to my world, Kent. And no, it won't go away."

Kent closed his eyes and sighed. "I'm sorry I put you through that. It sucks."

"It wasn't all bad. The awkwardness was worth still being involved in your life somehow."

There was another nod of his head. "I think I understand." He said softly.

"Remember after the store's opening night? When you got so drunk you grabbed onto Jen and told every man to back off because she was your w'man? You couldn't even say the whole word!"

Kent chuckled. "Yeah, I remember." There was a smile there for a moment. "Jen's friend called me the other day. Remember Miranda Walker from high school?"

"Miranda... No, what about her? Was it a booty call?"

"No. Apparently Jen did a lot of other things. Said she felt bad and heard what had happened." The smile faded.

"What are you talking about? What kinda things?"

"Apparently Jen was never really true. High school, college, after we were married. Guys, girls," he shook his head.

My jaw clenched. I looked at Kent and then looked away. How could I feel like Jen was the only wrong party? I'd made love with Kent twice when they were together.

"Apparently it wasn't just on me either. She mentioned one of your boyfriends."

"Yeah, Dave..."

"No. The one you walked in on in college. Said she told her she didn't know how you didn't know it was her. Made it easier since you didn't recognize her."

I blinked at him. "Will?" My eyes glazed over a little as I replayed the memory in my mind's eye. I let out a humorless chuckle. "Oh my god," my eyes came back to Kent. "Wh—I don't get it. Was she just some super slut or something? Or did she have a personal vendetta against me?"

"She saw how close we were. I think she just wanted to fuck that up, and even then she got bored with me and went," he tried to find the right word, "adventuring. She still held that fucking jealous card."

I shook my head and looked down at my hands. "Once we got to college we barely saw each other anymore. I was trying to give you space," Not to mention I couldn't stand to look at the two of them, it hurt too much to see them together.

"That was when she really starting straying. That trip she went on to help her mom move apparently only took a day. She was gone for three. I don't know who she did and I don't care. Sometimes it makes me not feel so bad for—" the words stopped as the waitress dropped off their drinks. Kent took a big sip of tea.

I looked up to him. "Not feel so bad for what?" Did Kent have another girl? Someone I didn't know about?

Kent shook his head. "I can't," his cheeks were starting to show a blush.

I frowned at him, "You can't what?"

Kent's hand squeezed the glass of tea on the table. "Tell me, Elly. What would you have done if I had whispered your name?"

He couldn't look at me. I felt the air leave my lungs, felt the color begin to fill my cheeks as I moved between shock and anger. "You..." I could barely hear my own voice as the implication of what he was saying moved through my mind.

"Do you hate me? Do you hate that I woke up with that going

on, and then I figured out it was real? I almost whispered your name." Kent shook his head and sighed as he pushed the sweet tea away from him on the table.

I opened my mouth to speak but I couldn't. I couldn't get any words out, his confession choked me. I ran away from the table before my tears blinded me.

I was pacing by the outdoor fountain in the little paved area between the Japanese restaurant and the movie theater when Kent walked slowly towards me. When he was a few feet away he spoke calmly. "Elly."

I looked at him and shook my head, a frown on my face. "Don't you fucking dare..."

"That has been weighing on me for a long time. I couldn't hold it in anymore." He held my water bottle in his hand. "I understand if you don't want to see me. I understand if you hate me, just know that I realize what I should have done." He set my water bottle down on the fountain but it was the furthest thing from my mind when I exploded.

"What you should have done?! That's just... That's great, Kent. What should you have done? Told your best friend the truth all those years ago?! That you're a fucking liar? I came back the next morning and you acted like nothing had happened when you knew—You knew how I felt about you? What had happened between us? And you just... You just went on. But how can I be surprised really when you fucked me two nights before you got married to her. Did you remember that in the morning too?" I didn't give him a chance to answer me, "Of course, you did. Did you feel pity for me? Is that why you did it? Poor little Elly, can't find a man... Just..." I put my hand up and then shook my head, I couldn't look at him. "I don't want to talk about this. It was a mistake. Both of those times were a huge mistake." I stepped away again, heading in the opposite direction of my apartment.

I felt Kent grab my wrist, stopping me. "No. They were not mistakes. I had just slept with my friend even though I was dating someone else. I felt crushed. It was my fault. I made you a cheater and not stopping it made me no better than Jen. That night of the bachelor party. That was the best night of my whole life. I've had lots of those with you, but that was up until we started playing the video games. All I remember are flashes here and there, but those didn't come until much later. Years later. Candles. Kisses. I was drunk, but when I got up I had realized something had happened. Again, I'd failed. I was getting married in two days and I'd just seduced my best friend, again! I know it was me. You can hold your alcohol so much better than I can."

"Spare me." I spit at him, pulling my wrist away from his grip. "I don't want to hear about how sorry I should feel for you because you couldn't keep your dick in your pants."

His shoulders fell, he shook his head and closed his eyes. "I spent too long fighting with Jen over the bullshit, over the lies. I don't want to do that with you."

"Great. Then let's not. Let's just go back to the way it was, let's just pretend this never happened and that shit never happened. Let's just have a fake friendship, a surface one. A happy-go-lucky friendship that isn't really a friendship at all. That works for me." I pasted on that smile that didn't reach my eyes, which were surely hideous from my tears mixing with my mascara. "See you at Thanksgiving, Kent. Maybe before then."

I walked away from him.

Chapter 20

It had taken me a long time to get myself out of bed the morning of Thanksgiving. I was not looking forward to putting a happy face on for the better part of an afternoon. I'd booked the band a gig just so I'd have a valid excuse to leave early in case things didn't go well.

A sense of dread filled me as I stepped up to Mrs. Lytle's doorstep. I opened the door and stepped inside. The house was filled with the savory smells of the large bird in the oven and roasting vegetables. I followed the source of the smell and found myself in the kitchen. Our mothers were in there, discussing the next recipe they were working on. I looked around but didn't see Kent.

They caught sight of me and came forward, hugging me tightly at the same time. "Elly! Come in and stay awhile," my mom said, motioning to my shoes.

"Sorry. I was just so drawn in by the delicious smells." I kissed them both on the cheek and then made my way back to the front door. As I removed my last shoe, the door opened behind me and a large gust of cold air rushed over my ass, making me shiver.

I stood up and saw Kent behind me, his eyes fixed firmly on my ass. "See something you like?" He opened his mouth to respond but I held up my hand to stop him. "Never mind. Don't answer that. Take your shoes and stuff off or you'll get yelled at like I just did." Before he could say anything I went into the kitchen, searching for a bottle of wine. I was going to need something to get me through this awkwardness.

There was a red already open on the counter. I poured two glasses and smiled as I sipped at one. "Kent and I will be in the living room. Let us know if you need any help with anything." I blocked his way as he came towards the kitchen and held one of the glasses up to him. "For you. Come pretend to watch TV with me." He followed without a word, sitting down beside me on the loveseat. I took another sip, grabbed the remote and flipped through the channels until I found the Macy's Thanksgiving Day Parade.

"Elly, I feel really bad ab—" I cut him off before he could go further down that road.

"I'm not here to talk about that. If you mention it again I'm going to make myself throw up in the bathroom and go home." I looked at him and slapped on a smile. "Just pretend we're happy sitting here together. And don't talk about that."

He sighed and turned his attention back to the TV. "What the hell is that?"

A cartoonish male figure with brown hair dressed in red and white floated down the street. I pointed to the title beneath the figure: "It's the Elf on the Shelf."

"What the hell is that?" His eyebrows were pinched together as he tried to decode it.

I laughed softly as I drank more of my wine. "Some Santa-trickery for little kids, I think."

He looked at me and gasped, "What do you mean 'Santa-trickery'? What are you saying?"

I held tightly onto my glass of wine, "Kent. It's probably time you know... Santa... Isn't... Real."

His face was one of mock-horror and I laughed so hard I almost spilled my wine all over his mother's couch. We made fun of the Macy's Thanksgiving Day Parade for hours, refilling our wine glasses twice. It was so nice feeling comfortable with him again. It was like old times and I had forgotten, momentarily, all about him trying to kiss me and his recent pronouncement of love.

After dinner, which was also lots of fun, probably due to the three glasses of wine I'd consumed, I made my way to the door. "I'd love to stay, guys, but I need to get to work."

"Elly, you work too much! Tell her, Kenny," his mother said.

He shrugged his shoulders and nodded. "It's true. You work too much. You should marry me and then you can live the sweet life." The room was silent as his words moved between all of us.

I shook my head, barely. I couldn't believe he'd just say that. Joking or not, it wasn't funny. I swallowed down my embarrassment. "I guess you forgot I'm not interested in marrying you." I watched his expression crumple into hurt.

I heard my mother gasp somewhere behind Kent. "Elly, that's not nice. What has gotten into you?"

"I've had too much to drink, I guess, Mom. My apologies for my loose tongue. I'd better go before I say anything else that would offend." I pulled my gaze from Kent and put my boots on. I was out the door before I put my coat on and inhaled deeply once I was outside. The door didn't shut as I'd expected it to and I turned around. Kent was there, a dark look on his face.

I walked down the steps, putting distance between us. "Go back inside, I don't have anything to say to you."

"What happened to us being friends?"

"I said pretend friends. And I'd ask you the same question. Marry you?" I scoffed and looked back, he was still following me. I stopped and turned around to face him. He didn't stop, he kept coming, his hands gripping my shoulders as his eyes roamed over my face. I wasn't scared of him hurting me. But it was a little scary feeling the strength he had over me.

"Is that really such a crazy thought?" he asked, his jaw worked under his skin.

"Yes. Go back inside. You're drunk."

He chuckled as he let me go. "No, Els, I'm not drunk. Not yet." He released me as he turned away and walked back inside. It took me an extra minute to compose myself after his form disappeared. Shit. Was this friendship thing going to work? I texted Stacy and walked as I waited for her and Rio to come pick me up.

Chapter 21

After the gig was over Bryan pulled me to the side and whispered in my ear, "I think I see my boss at the bar. And I think he's been glaring at me all night."

I turned my gaze to the bar, shielding my eyes from the spotlights to get a good look. It was. It was Kent. What the hell was he doing here?

"Do you want me to go talk to him?" Bryan asked, his hand on my lower back.

I shook my head slowly, "No. I'll just go get his keys and get him home." I turned towards him and kissed him softly. "Happy Thanksgiving."

His beautiful eyes smiled down at me, his fingers on my lower back clutching me into his chest a little tighter. "Happy Thanksgiving."

James and Rio were already headed for the table Stacy had reserved for them. Their post-show beers were waiting. I made my way over to the bar, preparing myself for the worst. "Kent, hey." I tapped him on his shoulder and he spun around, a grin on his lips when he saw that it was me.

"Elly-poo. I missed you. I didn't think you were going to come say hi. Since we aren't friends or anything."

I had to take a step back, his breath heavily laced with whiskey. I looked at the bartender and pointed to Kent and then made a cutting motion with my hand. Kent should've been cut off three drinks ago. I stepped between him and the guy next to him and called to the bartender, "Close his tab, please." I turned my face and Kent's was there, his lips so very close to mine. I pushed him back and frowned. "Kent, give me your credit card."

He chuckled and shook his head. "Nope. Only my friends or my wives get my credit card."

I sighed and pushed him back as he started to lean towards me. "Kent, you're ridiculous. Stand up."

He did, wobbling a little. "Ooh, little bossy Elly is back. I missed her."

I shook my head as I shoved my hands into his pockets, looking for his wallet. Of course it was in the last pocket I'd searched. His hands had moved to my hips to steady himself as I searched him. I grabbed his credit card and shoved it towards the bartender. I watched Kent out of the corner of my eye, he was bending over slowly towards my neck. I put my hand on his chest to hold him up. I felt it rumble under my fingers.

The bartender brought me the check and I scribbled Kent's name and then grabbed the card and let him go just long enough to shove his card back into the sleeve of his wallet, fold it up, and force it back into his pocket. His lips met with my collarbone.

"Kent, come on." I grabbed his hand and ducked away from him, tugging him towards Stacy's table. She looked at us with wide eyes when we approached, a beer to her lips.

"Hey, Elly. Hey, Kent," she said after she'd set her beer down. Rio was glaring at Kent as his arms came around my waist from behind, his chin resting on my shoulder. I rolled my eyes and tried to pull Kent's arms away from my waist. James's brow puckered as he tried to figure out what was going on.

"Hey. He's had too much to drink. I'm going to drive him home," I said.

"You sure that's a good idea?" Rio piped up and raised a questioning brow.

"Not really, but I don't trust him not to puke in the cab. I'll just throw him in the back, it'll be fine."

Rio stood up, "I'll go with you."

I shook my head, "N—" I froze as Kent's lips accosted my neck again. His hands wandered up to my ribcage and then suddenly they were gone. I turned around in time to see Bryan pushing Kent down to the floor with his fist to his face. I gasped and tried to move forward but a different male arm was around my waist, holding me back. "Bryan! Don't!"

Kent was on the ground, a hand to his cheekbone. "Fuck, Bryan. That's going to fucking hurt in the morning."

"You're lucky it wasn't your fucking balls. Keep your hands off of her," Bryan snapped.

I tried again to get in the middle but James squeezed me and spoke in my ear, "Don't want you getting a black eye trying to break up a fight, baby. Your pretty face is probably the only reason we get paying gigs." I ignored James semi-compliment. I couldn't take my eyes off the scene before me.

Kent got up off the floor slowly. He stumbled a little and then turned to look at Bryan. "You're right. I should keep my hands to myself. But I'm feeling pretty frisky tonight." Kent swung at Bryan mid-word and it landed on his left eye.

"Oh shit," James said near my ear, his grip loosening just enough for me to get away. "Elly!" he growled but he wasn't as fast as I was. I put my arms around Bryan's waist and tried to pull him back. He pulled my arms off of him and went at Kent again but Rio stopped him this time.

"Dude, chill. We haven't gotten paid yet." Bryan shrugged Rio's hand off his shoulder and walked away, still seething. I was torn, not sure which way to go. Kent was holding his already bruised cheek, his eyes on Bryan's retreating back.

Rio followed after Bryan and James stood by me and Stacy. Stacy stood up and went to Kent, putting an arm around his waist tentatively. "Good fight, Kent. But we should probably get you home now. Huh, tiger?"

"I fucked her, Bryan!" Kent yelled with a grin on his face. I gasped and watched as Bryan turned on his heel and came at Kent again, faster. Pure fury on his face.

"Stacy, goddamnit, get away from him!" Rio yelled as Bryan charged forward.

I stepped in front of him but he pushed me away, "Get the fuck out of the way!" I landed against James's chest and watched with hurt eyes as Bryan made a move to punch Kent again. Kent, however, now had matched fury, not mirth, in his eyes. He rammed his shoulder into Bryan's chest, throwing them both onto the nearest table. Beer bottles and pretzels went flying everywhere.

I looked away as the punches started to land again. Stacy grabbed me and we moved out of the bar, letting the bouncer and the boys sort it out.

"Oh my god," I said to Stacy, my vision blurred from the tears.

"They're both being assholes, Elly. Let's go to Rio's van. We'll wait for everything to cool off."

I nodded slowly as she led me there. I sat in the passenger's seat and stared at the front door of the bar. Bryan stormed out first and made his way to his car. His tires peeled as he sped out of the parking lot.

"Well, he's alive," Stacy said, trying to sound chipper for my sake. I had no words. He'd pushed me and I wasn't sure if it had been in anger at me or at Kent. Did he think that I'd slept with Kent as Kent had implied? Did Kent just ruin my chance at a good relationship? Was he really that vindictive? It was a side of him I'd never seen before. A side to both of them that I'd never seen before.

Kent stumbled out of the bar, alone. James and Rio were behind him, watching to make sure he didn't hurt himself, I guessed. He stumbled into the backseat of his car and James closed the door behind him.

I pulled out my phone and dialed his mother. He was going to need someone to make sure he was okay and it sure as hell wasn't going to be me after the stunt he'd just pulled in there.

Chapter 22

It had been a week since the incident after Thanksgiving and I still hadn't heard anything from Bryan. He had cancelled band practice and Kent said he'd been MIA at work. I was dressed and ready to go to his house when my apartment buzzer sounded.

"Hello?" I released the button after I was done speaking and applying my lip gloss as I waited.

"It's Bryan. Can I come in?" My lips were frozen, pressed together, as I contemplated what this meant. Had he come to apologize or tell me he'd found someone else? I wasn't really sure which one I wanted.

"Come on in." I buzzed him in and then opened the door after discarding the lip gloss into the little blue dish on my tiny front hall table.

He approached slowly, his shoulders set back confidently. His eyes met mine and I felt the air leave my lungs, he was as gorgeous as ever. The shiner that Kent had given him had almost disappeared, just a little trace of ugly yellow under his left eye. I stepped aside and he came in, looking around.

"You know we've been dating for a while and this is the first time I've actually seen the inside of your place."

I let out a little chuckle as I looked around. Truth be told, it wasn't much to look at. The one bedroom apartment was tiny but it served its purpose as a place for me to sleep, eat and store all my clothes, which were neatly hung on rolling racks behind the white love seat.

"There's not much to see." He was still looking around and it gave me a moment to look him over. He looked good, perhaps a little tired. I motioned to the couch. "Please, feel free to sit down. Do you want anything to drink?"

He shook his head, "No, I'm good, thanks." He sat down on my couch making it look tiny as he stretched his arms out along the back of it. His eyes looked up at me expectantly.

I mentally nudged myself and moved to sit down next to him in the little bit of space he left for me. "So what brings you here?"

He put his hand on my shoulder, his thumb slowly stroking it as he glanced down at me. "You. I've missed you."

I nodded slowly. "Oh?"

He nodded back and moved his body towards mine slowly, bringing his face closer to mine. "Oh…" I closed my eyes when his lips touched mine. His kisses still ignited a fire in my belly despite what he'd said a week earlier. I squeezed my fists together tightly and then reached up, pushing him away before he had me on my back.

"Bryan, wait." He moved his lips to my neck, kissing his way up to my ear slowly. "We have to talk about what happened."

He whispered into my ear, causing shivers, "I'm sorry, Elly." He continued to kiss my neck, drawing a moan from me as his hand moved to my breast, teasing my nipple. "I was an asshole, I said things I didn't mean. I was just so angry. I know you could never do any wrong. You're perfect." I gasped when his hand moved from my breast to the waistband of my skirt. I pressed my legs together as the heat and wetness gathered there.

I let it happen, I let his hands, lips and tongue roam my body. He assumed everything was forgiven. He made love to me on my couch, slow and sensual. He whispered about how beautiful I was, how he wanted me, how sorry he was. He made promises for the future. And I believed him. Every single word.

We had sex several more times that evening and in the morning he reluctantly left. He kissed me goodbye and got into his car, heading for home. He had a job interview to get to. I watched him drive away and was reminded by my stomach's loud roar that I hadn't eaten in a while. I quickly showered and then headed to the market.

* * *

The store was unusually crowded for a weekday morning. People were milling around me, trying to get what they needed as quickly as possible. I was stuffing apples into a clear plastic bag, humming softly in my post-coital glow. I gasped softly when I saw tattooed arms come around my shoulders from behind. But the fear quickly dissipated, knowing those tattoos belonged to Rio. His large arms lifted me just a little from the ground. I let out a little yip and turned around to face him when my feet were safely back on the floor. "Hey, big brother." My grin faded when I looked over his somber face.

The big bear of a man let his hands fall to his sides. His eyebrows furrowed slightly with what seemed to be a bit of confusion. "Who," He shook his head, "I mean, how ya doing, girlie?"

My grin was back due to his little joke. "I'm fine. Is there a reason why I wouldn't be fine?" I reached out and gently jabbed his bicep with my curled fist.

He shrugged his shoulders and then scratched at the back of his head. He had something he wanted to say but he knew I wasn't going to like it. "Just... No reason. You know me, Big Bro has to worry about you all the time."

I narrowed my gaze on him. "You're lying."

"It's nothing, dude. Don't worry about it."

I reached out and flicked him on his right thigh, close to his business. He jumped and slapped my hand away. "Hey! No touchin' the goods."

"Spill it, Rio! What the hell do you know?"

He sighed and scratched the back of his head again. "I ran into Bryan..."

"Oh? When? Just now?" I looked around the crowded market, wondering if he was there.

He shook his head and looked around, as if Bryan might come

out of nowhere and surprise us. "No, I ran into him the other night."

I shrugged, "Okay, and...?"

He put a hand on my shoulder and crouched down to look me in the eye. "I'm not here to stir up trouble, Elly. Much less say anything to hurt you. You know that."

I rolled my eyes as I pushed his hand off my shoulder. I was a big girl, dammit. "Oh my god, Rio! You're not doing very well with ripping off whatever band-aid I have on my nuts."

He threw his hands up, shaking his head. "You know what? This was a bad idea. Just forget I said anything." He turned away from me.

I dropped the bag of apples on top of the loose ones, "Uh-uh!" I followed after him, grabbed his arm and ran in front of his path. "Not so fast."

The muscles of his jaw tightened. "I saw Bryan at Trix the other night."

I reached up and grabbed his face, holding him by his ear, pulling him down until he was almost eye to eye with me. "Jesus, Rio. Just spit it out. I'm a big girl, I swear to God, I'll be okay. What happened? What did he say?"

He nibbled nervously on his lip ring and then spoke, "It wasn't what he said, it was who he was with. It was Siobhan."

I nodded and let him go, crossing my arms protectively over my chest. "He probably just ran into her and started catching up."

He sighed again and then pulled out his phone. He messed with it for a minute and then turned it so I could see it. It was a movie. I frowned at the phone but pressed play anyway. Even in the crowded store I could hear the thumping of the bass in the club. The camera was focused on Bryan and Siobhan. They were kissing each other rather passionately while Bryan's hand roamed over her. His hips pressed against hers rather roughly, Siobhan's leg was wrapped around his waist as he kept her pressed against the wall. I felt the energy leave me and I shook my head in disbelief.

"I... Why...why would he come crawling back to me last night if he'd just...?" I looked at Rio for the answer.

"Siobhan has a man, Elly. Not for long, I suspect, but for now she does. I guess he was just biding his time until she is single again?" Rio's eyes moved over me before settling on my face. "I'm sorry, Elly."

I scoffed, "Don't be sorry for me. Be glad that I found out now."

"As much as I don't want to admit it, I had hoped that it was you, though I don't like to think about you doing that." His face scrunched up in disgust which pulled a laugh from me. "Let me give you a ride home, kiddo?"

"Thanks." I sighed, already plotting what I was going to say to his punk-ass when I spoke with him next.

He put his large arm around my shoulder and led me to the parking lot where his beat-up Ford Taurus was waiting. I still held his phone in my hand and I sent the movie to my phone. I put his phone on his thigh and looked out the window as he drove the short distance to my apartment.

"So, I guess we need to find a new lead guitarist, huh?"

"Nope. If he wants to confront us and puss out he'll have to do it himself."

"Fair enough. We'll see if he's man enough to show up for practice." I winced as his grip tightened on the steering wheel; his knuckles white.

"Are you going to punch him?"

"I sure as hell want to."

I smiled and looked out the window, "I think you're going to have to share with James."

"How'd Bryan get that shiner anyway? He'd never tell me. I liked to think it was you, but I know better."

"What do you mean you know better? I'd totally hit him."

"I never said you wouldn't hit him, I just doubted you'd leave a mark like that on him."

He was teasing me. I grinned and shrugged my shoulder. "Pft. Whatever. Kent hit him." I said softly, crossing my arms over my chest again.

"Lucky bastard. I might get the chance yet." We arrived at my apartment and he put the car in park.

I looked over at him, "We weren't together, I don't think." I put my head back and looked at the parachute ceiling, it was going to fall down any day now. "Kent kind of, he um…"

"Hey. You don't have to tell me what happened. I'm just glad someone punched that jackass." I felt his large warm hand come to rest on my knee. "I'm sorry, Elly."

I looked away. Did everyone know how much of an asshole he was except me? I sniffled softly and reached for the door handle. I didn't want him to see me cry.

I made it to the door before I heard his brakes squealing in agony as he did a three-point turn and headed for the highway.

Chapter 23

Once safely inside my apartment, I pulled out my phone.

ME: HEY. HOW DID YOUR INTERVIEW GO?

BRYAN: GREAT. I EXPECT I'LL GET A JOB OFFER BY THE END OF THE WEEK.

ME: I RAN INTO RIO AT THE GROCERY STORE.

BRYAN: YEAH? HOW'S HE DOING? WAS HE PISSED WE MISSED PRACTICE THIS WEEK?

ME: HE'S GOOD. WE NEED TO PRACTICE THIS WEEK FOR OUR GIG NEXT WEEKEND. WHAT TIME IS GOOD FOR US TO MEET AT YOUR PLACE?

BRYAN: I'M FLEXIBLE, I'VE GOT NOTHING GOING ON.

ME: GREAT. WE'LL COME OVER TOMORROW NIGHT THEN.

BRYAN: COOL. AND HOW ABOUT YOU? ARE YOU COMING OVER TONIGHT?

ME: I DON'T THINK SO.

BRYAN: WHY NOT? I'M GOING TO MISS YOU.

My cheeks were flaming as I attached the video and then sent it to his phone. I waited for a few minutes and then hurled my phone to the floor. I was not going to be used as his place card until Siobhan decided she wanted him back. I was a lot of things, but that was not one of them.

I threw on my running clothes and ran until I was utterly

exhausted. I came home and showered, then picked up my phone to see if Bryan had replied. Two missed phone calls and voicemail were waiting for me.

I pushed play on the voicemail and held the phone to my ear, "This should be good," I muttered.

"Elly, alright, I don't have an excuse. I'd been talking to Shiv for a few days and she wanted to go out, so we did. It's exactly what you saw." There was a pause. "It's who I am."

I pulled back the phone and sat down on the bed, digesting his message. He was a Siobhan-fucker? Or an asshole? Or a player? A lady's man? What exactly was he?

A liar.

I dialed my mom's number and put the phone to my ear with a shaking hand.

After a few rings she picked up, "Hello?"

"Mom? Do you have a minute?" I hated that my voice sounded weak and vulnerable.

"Of course I do. What's wrong?" I heard moving and shifting on her end of the phone.

"Mom, what's wrong with me? Why do I pick such losers?"

"We all make mistakes. Sometimes you have to make a lot of mistakes before you finally find what you're looking for."

"Do all men cheat...?" Every single one that I knew had. Even Kent, as much as I hated to admit it to myself.

"No, not all of them..." she said softly.

"Most of them?"

"No, Elly."

"I just... I don't know if I want to be in a relationship again. It doesn't seem worth it."

"You know better than that. I said the same thing several times myself, but I found someone that changed that." The phone shifted briefly and her voice was thrown outwards. "Just shuffle up, I'll be there in a little while." She was talking to someone else.

"Mom, I'll let you go... I didn't mean to interrupt your game with

Kent's mom." I assumed that's who she was talking to, anyway.

"No, he can wait. His mom had an appointment so Kent came to sit in with me." I bolted upright.

"Oh god, Mom. I gotta go." I didn't want Kent to even get a little hint of what I was talking about with mom.

"Elly, he can't hear you. He's in the other room." I heard the frown in my mom's voice.

"He's smart and he has good ears. He'll put the pieces together and I don't want him to know that I'm still a loser, okay? I need to keep a little of my dignity."

"A loser? Elly, you're not a loser. And he knows it too. He spent the last hour telling me how terrific he thinks you are." My mom chuckled but I didn't think it was funny; not at all. Especially considering what Kent had done to me.

"Mom! Oh, God. You should tell him to get friends that are his own age. Unless you two have a Mrs. Robinson thing going on…"

"I don't have a chance with him, Elly. He's in love, and—"

I cut her off, "Don't say it! Don't. He's a cheater too, Ma. And a liar. Just don't get your hopes up where he's concerned. I'm not going to be with him, okay?"

"It's too late for that. They've been raised to the roof since you two were young whippersnappers."

"Have you been drinking?"

"Maybe a few glasses of wine."

"Great. I'll talk to you later, Mom."

"Elly…" She shuffled on her end again, "Oh, okay Kent. Thanks for coming by, tell your mom I missed her today and I'll see her next time." More shuffling and she whispered into the phone. "Elly, I think he might be headed your way!"

"Oh God. Bye Mom!" I hung up and looked at the time. It was almost dinner time. I quickly got dressed to go out and then headed out the door, walking the back way to the bars. On the way I called James and he agreed to take me out and help me wash away my sorrows. I knew he'd cheer me up, even if he didn't really mean any of the silly things he said. He was like a gay best friend; completely harmless.

I was sitting at the bar when I felt the familiar slap on my left thigh. James leaned in close and spoke into my ear. "Finally you've invited me to go slumming with you. I'll show you a good time, baby girl." He leaned back and waggled his eyebrows playfully.

I grinned and pointed to my glass which was already empty. "You're buying, right?"

"Hell yeah." He flagged down the bartender, ordering himself a beer and me another screwdriver. He turned back to me while we waited for our drinks, "So that tool picked Shiv over you?"

I shrugged. "She's got great boobies."

He nodded as he looked away. I could see him pulling up a mental image of her boobs. "Yeah she does." I laughed and nudged him with my elbow to knock him out of his boob trance. He grinned and looked at me. "But seriously, doll, so not cool. I'd take you over Shiv any day. You probably make all those pretty sounds that drive men like me wild in the sack."

I looked over his face, he was a handsome guy, but just not the one for me. I put my hand on his cheek, "You're going to find your girl, James. But she's not me."

"You think I don't know that? You're too good for the likes of me." He moved in slow and I thought for sure he was going to kiss me but his lips landed on my forehead instead. "Now quite this sappy shit and let's get wasted." His eyes moved over a trashy-looking lady at the other end of the bar. He lifted his beer to her with a grin.

I smiled and sipped my drink. "You can do better than that."

"Yeah, but I don't wanna do better than that tonight. Unless... You're offering?"

I grinned and shrugged. "You never know. Might happen around drink ten."

He grumbled and sipped his beer, "I'm not sure I can hold out that long."

I laughed softly, "So don't, goofball." I picked up the bar menu and flipped it over, looking for something to eat. Nothing looked that appealing. "Hungry?" I glanced at him and his raised eyebrow made me laugh. "Right... Forgot who I was asking. What do you want?"

"You buying, Princess?"

"Of course. I'll buy the food and you buy the drinks; seems totally fair to me." We ordered a plate of nachos and two burgers. We were halfway through the plate of nachos when James started cussing up a storm. I was on my third shot and feeling pretty damn loose. I tried to look around him and fell back, laughing as my ass crashed against the floor.

James hopped off his stool and picked me up. He put his arms around me, his hands starting to grope my ass. I giggled and tried to push him away. "James, what are you doing?"

And then I heard Bryan's voice behind his back. "James, hey man. What's..." His voice trailed off as his eyes met mine. I grinned and wiggled my fingers in his direction. James pulled me into his side as he swung around to face Bryan.

"Hey dude, just chillin' with Elly." Siobhan was holding Bryan's hand. I started to laugh as Bryan's face started to turn red with anger and I turned my face into James arm to try to hide it. James pat my head.

"What the hell is so funny, Elly?" I dared a peek and started to bust out laughing again.

"I just... You're just..." I twirled my hair around my finger slowly as I wondered if Siobhan ever came with Bryan. I wasn't going to ask her but damn if I wasn't curious. "Hey Siobhan. How's it going?"

She nodded at me and offered a little smile, "I'm alright. How are you?"

"Drunk," I snickered. James grinned at my side and pulled me closer.

"She's just drinking off some dumb-ass." Bryan nodded, acknowledging that it was him James was referring to.

"We'll see you later, then." James nodded and waited until Bryan was turned around before calling out to him.

"Bryan?" When Bryan turned James drew back his fist and punched him in his other eye. Bryan fell back against Siobhan who absorbed his weight and then circled around him, her hands at his waist, trying to look at his injury.

I was drunk but I still gasped, shocked by the boy-on-boy violence. "James!" He didn't give Bryan time to recover and come back at him. He threw money on the bar, grabbed my hand and pulled me out of the building.

I glanced back to see Bryan staring at me with his good eye. Guess he messed with the wrong chick.

Chapter 24

After he kissed me goodbye on the forehead, James pulled away from the curb and headed for Rio's. Apparently James still wanted to punch something and Rio's gym was going to be the remedy for that.

I looked up at the stars: they moved in a circular motion and then cut sharply to the side as I staggered towards my apartment door.

Once safely inside my condo I pulled out my phone and texted Kent. He was the only one I could call. I knew that I wanted to be held and comforted. And I knew that Kent would be just the guy for the job. He said he loved me after all, so he could damn well prove it. If he could prove that he would be there for me, it might even help in repairing our friendship.

Ah, that was Kent. Always so reliable. Well, until a girl got involved, that is. I attempted to brush my teeth with my light head and I missed the drain. The spittle landed near the emergency water hole instead. I laughed it off. I was a little tipsy. I hoped I could hold it together. It had been awhile since I'd let myself go like this.

My thoughts went back to Kent as I fiddled around in the kitchen, opening up cupboards, looking for something toxic for my body. It was girl custom to binge on a pint of ice cream, wasn't it? I went to the fridge and opened it up. I was pissed and slightly more heart broken when I found there was nothing in there except some freezer-burned peas.

"Damnit." I opened the fridge and stared for a minute. If Kent and I did become friends again and he did find another woman it would just be the same. The same as before. He'd drag me on his stupid dates and make out in front of me while I pretended to be interested in something across the room. And his new girlfriend would probably be as much of a loser as the first one had been. I slammed the door on the fridge and went to the door in the rear of the kitchen. It lead to a patio the size of a bathroom stall.

I sat down in my pink plastic Adirondack chair and leaned my head back, looking at the stars again. They didn't move this time.

I was a grown woman now. I could easily say no. I had a life and I didn't need to protect him. And I didn't need to throw myself at him either. I wasn't interested. He was a cheater just like the rest of them. Monogamy just wasn't natural. Love was a sham. Not the kind you feel for your family or your friends. But the hot, sexy, can't-wait-to-spend-forever-together kind of love. That wasn't real.

I felt my eyes drifting closed and then the doorbell rang. I grumbled and pushed up from my chair, heading for the door. I opened it and Kent was there, a big red bag of Twizzlers in his left hand. He held them up and raised his eyebrows. "It's not delivery, it's your food dealer."

I grabbed the Twizzlers, "Thanks, put it on my tab." I put my hand on his wide, muscular chest and pushed him backwards. His hot hand came on top of mine and clasped it tightly.

"I don't keep tabs." He smiled softly, looking down at me with those deep brown eyes. I paused as he leaned closer and closer, and at the last second, the last agonizing second before I thought his lips were going to touch mine he was gone. He'd twisted by me and ran inside my apartment.

My heart was pounding and I took a minute to compose myself before turning around. I don't want to be his next wife. I'm just drunk, that's all. He was sitting on my couch, his limbs long and large and taking up most of it. "That was a little dirty, Kenny."

He shrugged his shoulder, half a smirk on his lips. "Payback is a bitch."

I closed the door behind me and held the Twizzlers tight against my chest. "I don't know what you're referring to." I did. I was mean to him all the time, especially growing up.

"No? You always wore those damn outfits around me. I'm not sure I could even name the last time you didn't play dirty, Els."

"What outfits?" He nodded to me, his eyes slowly taking in my tight dark denim jeans and my ivory crocheted babydoll cami top. I glanced down and laughed softly. "Whatever, Kent. This is not playing dirty. If I wanted to play dirty I'd have opened the door dressed in my underwear."

"Or naked," he said. I felt my face flush and turned away, heading for the kitchen. I did not want to be his wife. I was just drunk.

"Do you want something to drink?" The best way to keep his mind out of the gutter was to change the subject, I hoped. This flirty Kent was new to me. I grabbed some glasses and put them on the counter loudly. I was surprised by my own strength and equally impressed that the glasses didn't break.

He called out from the living room, "Dew would be awesome but since you probably don't have any, I'll take water."

I poured us both water and went back to the couch with them, slowly so I didn't spill. I nudged his knee with my foot, and when he moved over I took a seat next to him, holding out the water. "Cheers!"

He tapped his glass to mine as he studied my face. "So, I realize that I was totally shit-faced the other night and I need to apologize for what I did or said. I don't remember any of it." Isn't that convenient? He never remembered anything when he was drunk.

I shrugged my shoulders and reached forward, grabbing the remote. "It's fine. I'm sure you had my best intentions in mind when you punched Bryan in the face and lied to him by telling him you fucked me. I mean technically you didn't lie. But you made it sound like we'd fucked recently and you and I both know it was a long, long time ago. Ancient history that probably shouldn't even be mentioned. Ever." I flipped on the TV and then set the remote on my thigh.

"Did you talk to him?"

"Who?" I know I was playing stupid but I needed time for my drunk brain to catch up.

"Bryan." I kept my eyes on the TV but I felt the couch move as he shifted next to me.

"Oh, um... Yeah." I glanced at him, his body was turned towards me, he wasn't interested or watching the TV at all. But I was... Or at least pretending to.

"And? Are you two still together?"

"Not so much." I glanced, catching his hand running roughly through his hair.

"Shit, Elly. I'm sorry." I shook my head and pat him on his knee.

"No. Don't be sorry. It wasn't because of what you said. He was an asshole unworthy of me, just like all the others." I refused to look at Kent. I didn't want him to even catch the slightest hint that I was hurting inside. I started flipping through the channels, trying to distract myself from my thoughts. The thought of Bryan, being inside Siobhan, and the next night being inside me. Bryan using me as a place card, waiting for his 'true love' to come around again, was constantly trying to replay in my mind.

I was mid-button pushing when the remote was taken from my hand. I opened my mouth to protest but a warm mouth pressed against mine, stealing it. It was a soft, tender kiss and when Kent pulled back he whispered, "I'm sorry, Elly."

"For kissing me?" I asked softly, my eyes meeting his. He shook his head softly, barely noticeable.

"No. Because you're hurting. I don't want you to hurt anymore." As I stared at his face, his handsome face, I wondered what it would be like to be with him while he was sober and conscious.

"Have you had any flashbacks or felt anything weird since your head injury?"

"No." He said it softly, his breath warming my lips. I watched as his eyes lowered to my lips as I bit myself gently, wondering if I should just do it—Just live in the moment.

He was still divorced, I was newly single. Who were we going to hurt if we...? No one. I tilted my head back, my hand found the back of his neck and I pulled his lips to mine, moaning as he captured them, the kiss sizzled between us, heating both our bodies.

He pulled back, grabbed my water, and set both of them on the coffee table in front of us. "Elly, if it goes too far just tell me. Tell me to stop. I don't want to—" I cut him off with another kiss. He didn't seem to mind, his chest rumbled in satisfaction as he lowered himself onto me. His now-free hands explored my upper body, caressing me through my thin top. I arched my back when his warm thumb brushed over my nipple. It puckered at his touch, wanting more.

This man was amazing; everything my teenaged fantasies hoped he would be. As his mouth appeased mine, I felt my body start to smolder. Kissing was not enough, but I didn't want to stop. Kissing him felt like heaven.

His skillful fingers dipped between us, undoing my jeans. After ripping everything off my lower limbs, he hooked his hands beneath my knees and pulled me so that I was horizontal on the couch. His dark eyes sparkled with lust as he settled his face between my thighs. "So fucking perfect. I'm looking forward to doing this sober, to remembering every detail for the rest of my life. You are perfect, Elly." He took his first lick and a moan ripped through me. He moaned too. "As good as I remember..." That was the last thing he said before he buried his head between my thighs. My orgasm took me quickly—too quickly—I wanted him to worship me that way forever.

As I panted softly, recovering he stood up and looked down at me. "I want to do that to you every day for the rest of my life." He wiped my juices from his mouth with the bottom of his shirt and then picked me up, I gasped when my sensitive center brushed against him. I wrapped my arms and legs around him as he carried me to my bedroom. I had no words for him. I wasn't sure what to say.

"Thank you." It was all that came to my sex-fuzzed, drunken mind.

He grinned just before lowering me onto the bed, his body still over mine. There was something there in his eyes, but I wasn't sure if it was love or just a lust-gleam.

As he filled me that night, over and over again, my walls came down. My body, my heart filled with love. Love for what he could do to me; the things he could make me feel. Before my sated, sweaty body fell asleep I was sure I heard him ask me to marry him.

Chapter 25

I stretched with a smile. That dream was really good, I hadn't had one like that in years. I rolled over and my hand met with a hard, warm chest. My attempt to sit up was foiled by his large hand encircling my waist, turning me and pulling me back against his body. I looked over my shoulder and blinked as my eyes took in Kent's face, his eyes still closed. I wiggled my toes and realized that we were both very much naked. Naked like the day we were born. I gently picked up his arm and tried to scoot away but that only made him snuggle me closer.

He groaned and nibbled on my ear. "Elly, a little longer."

I froze. Shit. It wasn't a dream—It was real. The reality of it hit me, and then I relaxed a little. A smile on my lips. It was Kent. He would be totally cool with—I winced. He wouldn't. He wouldn't be cool with us being friends with benefits... Would he? I seriously doubted it.

"I have to use the bathroom," I mumbled softly. He groaned again but let me go. I slipped off the bed and retreated like a coward into the bathroom.

As I waited for the water to warm up I brushed my teeth and thought about what I was going to say to him. How could I bring it up without hurting his feelings? Was there a way? He would find another woman soon enough and leave me devastated, again. And I couldn't put our friendship through that again. When it happened I would lose him forever because it would be too hard to know him that way and then lose him to another woman. I did not think I could recover from that.

After the shower I stepped into my bedroom and found Kent laying on my bed, his arms coming down after a large yawn, his dark eyes on me. I pulled the towel tighter around my chest and smiled. "Hey, sleepy head, are you gonna lay there all day?"

He nodded his head, flashing me with a sleepy grin, "Of course. I was hoping you could join me."

My feet felt like big blocks of cement. I had to admit to myself that it was a tempting offer as my eyes roamed slowly over his naked chest and his powerful arms. "Don't you have a store to run?" I dropped my gaze and turned, forcing my feet to move. I opened my drawers and rustled around for something to wear.

"I do, yeah, but staying in bed just sounds so amazing right now."

I grabbed a couple of shirts and slammed them back into the drawer in frustration. Dammit, where was that goddamn sweatshirt?! I bent down and moved onto the bottom drawer, rifling through it, determined to find it. I vaguely heard Kent speaking behind me.

"You want to come back to bed for a little bit?" I paused and turned, looking around my hip. He was staring directly at my bare ass. I stood up quickly, the edge of the top drawer scraping against the back of my head. I whimpered, stood up straight and put my hand to the spot I swear was bleeding.

"Shit, Elly, I'm sorry. You all right?" I heard rustling and felt his body come up behind mine.

"Fine, I'll be fine." I checked my hand to see if there was blood on it and there wasn't. I stayed where I was, my back still to him, I knew as he wrapped his arms around me that he was naked, could feel the press of his dick against the small of my back.

He pressed a kiss to my bare shoulder and whispered, "Darn. I was kind of hoping I could play doctor."

I shivered involuntarily and closed my eyes, trying to block out the yearning. I wanted so badly to play doctor with him but I couldn't let him distract me. "Kent..." I whispered softly. God dammit if he didn't feel good against my back, like I fit with him. One of his hands came up and wrapped around the hand that was clutching the front of my towel for dear life and his lips caressed my neck. I fought back a groan, I had to make this stop or go faster, I wasn't sure which. "How would you feel about being friend with benefits? Like an open relationship kind of thing?"

That did it. He released his hold on me and took a step back, I heard the air leaving his lungs in a rush; I'd stunned him. "That..."

I refused to turn around and stare at him. I continued to rifle through my drawers. If he was as shocked and hurt as I suspected, I didn't want to see it yet.

I heard the bed crinkle as he sat down on it, "Why would you want that? You're not that kind of girl."

I pulled on a white sweatshirt roughly. Maybe I wasn't that kind of girl before, but I was determined to be now. "I've had one bad relationship after another, I don't want to do that again." I grabbed some black leggings and pulled them on. When I turned around to look at him he was hunched over, his elbows on his knees, his hands in his hair, and he was staring at the floor.

He sat up abruptly and I could see his tongue pressing against the side of his cheek, "You're assuming it's going to be bad with us before you've even given me a chance." His eyes looked up to meet mine and I felt my insides melt and pool in my lower belly. "The sex between us is," he licked his lips before continuing, "amazing but I don't want to be that guy who comes over here, makes love to you all night and then leaves the next morning." He grabbed his boxers and yanked them on. "I want the whole thing, Elly."

I felt the frown on my face, "So it's all or nothing?"

He met my eyes and nodded. "All or nothing."

I felt my chest constrict and put my hands behind me to hold onto the dresser for support in case my heart decided to shut down on me. "So if I don't want to be in a committed sexual relationship with you you're just going to cut me out of your life altogether?"

"I don't want to cut you out. I," he paused as his eyes traveled very slowly down my body, his gaze alone making it sizzle and hum.

"You what?" I had to keep talking, to avoid throwing myself at him like a fool.

His eyes met mine as he continued, "I want to feel you against me at night. I want to take showers with you in the morning, cook you dinner. I want to go the movies and fucking hold hands everywhere we walk. Of course I want other things. I'm not going to be able to get last night out of my mind, but I want more than just sex."

He wasn't saying anything that couldn't be done under the cover of Friends-With-Benefits. I lifted my chin defiantly. "So why can't we do that? And be casual about it?"

"There's nothing casual about the way I feel about you."

"Right. The love thing again." I sighed and looked down at my toes. I couldn't see them for long before Kent's came into view. He caged me in with his arms and I painfully dragged my gaze up his practically naked body. If he had done this to me years ago I would've done anything he asked. But not anymore. I met his eyes.

"Don't tell me you don't feel something," he said.

"I feel like I have good sex with my friend." I wasn't about to stroke his ego and admit the sex was fucking stellar. "That's what I feel."

"The sex isn't good because it's sex. There is more there. The feelings add to the experience."

I almost laughed. He'd had sex with two women in his life, who was he to counsel me about why the sex felt so great. "I didn't know you were a sex expert, Kenny."

He didn't think I was funny at all. He moved like a viper, quickly pressing his lips to mine. His left hand snaked under my shirt, his hand warm against my side. His kiss was fucking hot and delicious and I heard someone whimper. Vaguely, I was aware that it was me.

He broke the kiss and studied my face, "Tell me you didn't feel that." I was mesmerized by his lips, slightly swollen and wet from our kiss, "Tell me you didn't feel that excitement because it was me, and not just someone else." And then he did it again, he kissed me silly as I clung to the dresser behind me for dear life.

He pulled back again, "Tell me, Elly. Tell me you don't want it."

His arm slid around my back and pulled me to his body.

"I want your sex attention, yes. But I don't want to be your girlfriend." I didn't expect to see the pain so dramatically on his face, but there it was. And then it was gone, covered. He released me and went to pick up the rest of his discarded clothes.

I felt my knees quaking and I wasn't sure if it was from the kissing or the fear that this might be the last time I saw him.

As he dressed he spoke, "I gotta go, Elly." As soon as his clothes were on, he was gone.

Chapter 26

A week had gone by and I hadn't heard anything from Kent. I worked double shifts to keep myself from going to him but I'd worked so much that the boss gave me a couple of days off and refused me when I'd tried to come in.

Christmas was next week so I went shopping to try to fill the void, but everywhere I went I saw Kent, or I saw something I wanted to gift to Kent. Or I saw a couple, holding hands, smiling at each other like they were in love. Which was stupid because a month or a year from now that man was going to cheat on that woman and she would be shopping alone, just like me.

I was standing at the grocery store, staring at the strawberries which, thanks to globalization and world trading, were available in the middle of winter. He was probably regretting his hasty decision by now. He was probably having hot sex dreams about me just like I was. And it was probably killing him but he probably wanted to pout and try to save face. I was going to go over there and find out. I had nothing better to do and it was killing me not to know.

I knocked on his door an hour later with a bag full of stuff. He opened it, and while he was checking me out I stepped in, I didn't want to give him the chance to refuse me entry. It was much easier to bully your way into things where he was concerned. He didn't object so I kept walking to his kitchen, "I've got lots of goodies for us tonight!" I tried to sound cheery so maybe I could trick him.

I felt his presence behind me as I set the bag on his small counter and started to pull things out, "Strawberries and whipped cream. Mountain Dew and Diet Mountain Dew. Twizzlers. Ho-hos.

And some bacon for the morning. And, of course, a Redbox movie so we have something to watch." I crumpled up the plastic bag and set it next to the stuff. I went to him and put my arms around his neck, he seemed a little put off but he wrapped his arms around me just the same. "What do you want to do first?"

"Umm... Twizzlers and Redbox."

I stood on my toes and pressed my lips to his, trying to slowly melt his resolve and soften him up to the idea of me being in his space. I felt him start to harden before he pulled back. "Elly," he whispered.

I could see the restraint in his face, his body wanted me but his mind was fighting back hard. I pulled him close and kissed his neck softly. "I've missed you." I felt him shiver against my body and felt his dick harden some more against my belly.

"I wanted to hear you say that," he whispered.

My lips met his ear as I whispered softly, "That I missed you inside of me?" My hand slipped between us, grasping him in my hand. I heard the catch in his breath a moment before I felt his fingers close around my wrist. I wasn't about to let him think himself out of what I wanted to do. My body wanted his as much as his wanted mine. "Is that what you wanted to hear me say?" I grazed my teeth slowly down the side of his neck.

"I—," his breath stuttered.

"You?" I squeezed him through his jeans gently.

"I... Want more..." he forced it from between his lips.

"More what?" I moved my hands to the front of his jeans, slowly undoing them, hoping he wasn't going to reject me. He reached behind and put both hands on the counter, surrendering to me. I looked up into his dark eyes, a little smile on my lips. "You don't have to talk, it's fine. I'll talk for you." My fingers slid to his hips and pushed his jeans down slowly. "Elly, I want more of our bodies... Together. I want whatever you want because we're best friends," as I spoke I moved down his body, the last word whispered on the front of his tented boxers, "forever." His eyes were trained on me, watching as I came back up, grabbing his dick and pulling it slowly from his clothes. "Even if I don't want to be your girlfriend...?" I rubbed my thumb over the tip, "Yes, Elly. I want you however you'll let me have you." His eyes closed. "I'm glad we could come to an agreement, finally."

I moved away from him and washed the strawberries in the sink. I saw him from the corner of my eye stuffing himself back into his boxers after rubbing his face with his hands.

I grabbed the whipped cream and berries and moved towards the bedroom, "Coming?" I heard his footsteps as he followed me after a moment's pause. The plan was working. He was totally going to own my body tonight. I felt the tightness in my belly as I freed my hands and then stripped down to my panties and bra.

"So beautiful," I heard him hoarsely whisper from the doorway.

I looked at him over my shoulder, "If only you'd said that to me when I was fifteen." I laid down in the middle of his bed and waited for him to join me.

"I did," He wasted no time getting into the bed beside me, his pants loose, his shirt half unbuttoned.

"I only remember feeling like you were just being nice." I grabbed the whipped cream and shook it as I turned towards him, my free hand roaming over the warm hardness of his exposed chest. I loved how there was only a sprinkling of hair.

"No, not just nice."

"I know that now. You just wanted to use me to experiment with." I popped the cap off the bottle.

"It wasn't just experimenting, unlike you. What are you doing?"

"I'm having fun with my friend." I held the can upside down and pushed the side of the nozzle. A cold stream of cream sprayed onto his chest.

His inhaled sharply, his hands gripping the covers, "Cold!"

I grinned, "I'll make it better," I licked it off his chest slowly, kissing his skin as I went.

When I sat up he was chuckling at me and wiped at his nose, "You've got a little..."

I felt my cheeks flame as I wiped off the whipped cream, so

much for being sexy. "You want a turn?"

I held out the can and he took it. He turned it sideways and sprayed my chest at the bra-line. I closed my eyes when his body leaned over mine and I felt his tongue cleaning up. He made me feel things no other guy ever had.

I opened my eyes and took the can from him. "My turn." I reached down and pulled him from his boxers. I sprayed him and then bent down and sucked it off. I felt him shiver and heard the moan. The power I had over him warmed me inside.

He pulled me up and exposed my breasts. He applied the whipped cream to one nipple and then cleaned it off, leaving my core wet. I groaned and when he pulled back, I took the can and sprayed the other side. "Your turn again!"

"Gladly," he murmured before moving on to my other breast. His tongue darted out, tasted it and teased it before his mouth captured it and sucked. "You taste too sweet with the whipped cream." He tossed the can over the side of the bed and moved his kisses down the front of my body. I shivered as his lips caressed over me, his hair tickled me as he turned his head and grazed my thigh with his teeth. "You taste like honey. You smell incredible, I just want," I gasped as I watched him delve between my legs, his tongue anxiously lapping.

My hips raised up greedily as I held onto his hair, "You shouldn't be so... Good..."

He groaned and ate me out relentlessly, my body quivered and gushed as I released. He made me feel things, made me want to give myself to him fully just so I could feel that way every night for the rest of my life. As I struggled to get my mind back to a normal, sane place—one where Kent and I were not wearing golden rings, Kent moved off the bed and disrobed completely. I felt the tension between my legs as I stared at him. He was standing at full attention, bouncing slightly as he made his way back between my thighs. His hand explored my skin from hip to breast.

"Do you need some more attention?"

I slowly shook my head as my hips pressed upwards, teasing

him with my wetness. "I don't want you to get lock-jaw."

"It would take more than twice for me to get lock-jaw. You're so easy to please."

"Or maybe you're just that good."

He smiled at me, his eyes dark as he slipped his hands under me and rolled us over so that I was on top of him. "Sit on my face, or climb on my cock. Either way you're going again."

I looked down at him, my hands on his chest. I was hearing things, surely. "What did you say?"

"Sit on my face or climb on my cock." His hands were on my hips. He lifted me up, bucking me out of my shock.

"You have such a filthy mouth." It wasn't very fair that I was getting all the attention. I turned around so that my hips were above his head and his were aligned with mine. I didn't lower my hips, I stayed a safe distance from him as I took him into my mouth.

He loved it, his groan of pleasure vibrating the bed beneath us. Unlike the men in my past Kent let his hands roam over me, gently, slowly as if he were taking every inch of me into his memory.

His hands on my hips tried to pull me down to his lips, but I resisted and sat up, he popped out of my mouth.

"Hey, you're looking pretty tired back there."

"No, I'm not." He lifted his face, trying to get another taste. I slid off of him and got to the edge of the bed before he grabbed onto my arm, holding me there. "You're going to leave me hanging right now?" He eyes were still amused, which was good.

"Yeah. Do you mind?"

"I guess not. I'll just go get a cold shower and go to bed." He started to get up but I pushed him back onto the bed.

"No! You stay here. I'm getting the first shower."

He stayed but a grin was on his lips, the same lips that gave me such pleasure minutes ago.

I forced myself into the bathroom and while I was bent over I heard his voice in the doorway. "I'll never get tired of that view."

I glanced at him with a grin. "You should take a picture. It'll last you longer."

"Don't tempt me, woman. I'll go get a camera."

"Just promise me that you'll get paid a lot for it."

He chuckled and then sidestepped around me and into my hot shower.

"Hey! That's my shower."

"My shower now. You snooze, you lose." He chuckled as the shower curtain rings scraped across the metal of the curtain rod, shielding his fabulous body from my view.

I climbed in behind him and when I rubbed my hands over his back his hand went to the wall, bracing himself. I couldn't help it, my hand was like a magnet, drawn to his shaft. I clasped my hand around it and started to stroke, he was still hard from our foreplay.

His head was bent, his body shivering slightly as my slippery hand moved over him. "Do you like that?" He moaned and I wondered if I was hurting him so I slowed down.

His body jerked and he turned his head slightly, "Don't stop, It's... Fucking hot to watch."

That was all the encouragement I needed. I stroked him until he suddenly turned around and crushed my lips with his.

"I can't wait any longer."

He backed me against the shower wall, his hands went to my bottom and he lifted me. His kisses pummeled me while he put himself between my thighs.

"I won't deny myself of you, not tonight. I want something to keep me warm at night because I know you won't."

I opened my mouth to refute him but his hard length sliding into me stole away my words. My grip on him tightened and I felt him shudder, my body was tense in his hot hands.

He restrained himself, torturing both of us as he slid in and out, slowly. His lips scalded my skin and then left my body as he drew his head back to look at me.

I met his eyes and he watched as I fought to keep my eyes open while he made love to me. I dug into his shoulder with my nails, urging him to go faster. I wanted more, craved more. I wanted him to make the ache go away.

"Please?" I whispered.

He slowed down even more, making me feel every centimeter. I closed my eyes and put my head back against the cold stone tile.

"Please?!" I begged him.

"I'll give you whatever you want, Elly, you just have to ask me." I heard him groan, his eyes dropping to my mouth. I released my lower lip, which I hadn't realized I was biting quite so hard.

"Will you please go faster? Harder? I want to feel how much you want this."

He groaned again and pressed his lips to mine as he thrust all the way in hard, the sound of slapping skin echoed against the moist walls. A whimper escaped from my throat and I held on tight, my cheeks hot.

He let himself go then, copulating with me like a wild, half-starved man. It was animalistic, hot, and when it was all over I realized we'd both come, together. And I realized we hadn't used protection.

I made a mental note to go to the pharmacy as soon as I left after breakfast tomorrow.

I wasn't going to ruin what just happened by mentioning it.

As soon as I stepped out of the shower I heard my phone ringing. I picked it up and noted that it was my mother. Before I could accept the call she'd hung up. It was then I noticed the text messages, five from her in the last half hour.

I dialed my mother, clutching my towel to my chest, "Mom, hey."

She was upset, the devastation in her voice. "Elly, thank God! Are you with Kent? I can't reach him and—"

I interrupted her because she was getting herself worked up. "I'll find him."

"Get to St. Joseph's Hospital as quickly as you can. His mother was in a car accident. It's bad Elly just..."

Her voice faded and I felt the color drain from my face. "Okay, we'll be there. Hang tight."

I started to dress as Kent studied me. "Elly, you okay?"

"We have to go see my mom. Get dressed, okay?"

Chapter 27

With my instructions on where to go Kent drove us to the hospital. When we pulled into the parking spot he turned off the car and looked at me, I could feel the worry hanging in the air. The tension was thick.

"What's going on, Elly?"

"My mom is here. We need to go find her." I wasn't ready to tell him yet, I didn't even know the details of what to tell him.

My phone chirped, my mother texted me the room number. I unbuckled and got out of the car, Kent was shocked and it took him a few moments to catch up to me as I walked into the hospital.

"Is she okay? Oh my god, Elly." He grabbed my hand and I squeezed it tightly.

"She'll be okay." I couldn't look at him as I led him upstairs. As we approached the room we saw my mother and Jen standing beside a door.

Kent slowed and looked down at me, "What the fuck is she doing here? Elly, what's going on?"

I shook my head and spoke softly, looking up at him. "I don't know what she's doing here but I can guess the same thing we are... Your mom..." I saw his face pale.

Kent's hand left mine as Jen came between us, her arms wrapping around him, her sobs seeming to amplify as I stepped back to give them room. His hands wrapped around her, his eyes stared at the closed door where his mother was.

"This has got to be some kind of—"

Jen cut him off. "Joke? It's not." Jen took his hand and pulled him to the room. "Maybe she'll wake up if she knows you're here. The doctors are still hopeful that she'll wake up."

I held the door open, my mother standing next to me, her hand on my lower back for comfort. I watched as Kent approached his mother, whose head was wrapped in white gauze, her face bruised and her body lifeless. He reached for her hand and held it gently. "Mom? You can wake up now, Mom. I'm here..."

Jen looked at me and my mother and nodded, signaling that we should probably leave him and his sadness for now.

We waited for a few moments and I comforted my mother, letting her cry on me.

"We should probably get you home, you'll need your rest to come back and relieve Kent." My mother nodded and as we walked away I heard Kent's voice.

"Jen, you can go, I'm going to stay."

"Is there anything I can bring you, Kenny? A change of clothes? Coffee?"

"Elly!" His call stopped us and I turned to face him. He rushed over and held out his keys. "Can you get me some clothes? Please?" I nodded as I took the keys. The warmth of his fingers shocking me.

After I took the keys he disappeared back into the room with his mother. Jen smiled and shrugged. "I'll just stay here in case he needs anything else."

* * *

I arrived at the hospital a couple of hours later, Kent's gym bag in hand. I had successfully resisted the temptation to wrap myself in his ugly orange blanket and cry for a little while. Seeing him with Jen had hit me hard; they had history and I knew he'd loved her once. I also knew that those feelings didn't just disappear.

I peeked into his mom's room and saw Jen holding her hand. She was talking to her, comforting her. My heart dropped to my belly. Despite what he'd said to me, despite how much he claimed to hate her, here she was. With his mom.

I dropped the gym bag and quickly left the hospital before I crumpled to the ground and curled up in a fetal position. I'd opened myself up to him, let him past my walls just a little and he sliced me open again.

As I got into the car my phone chirped.

KENT: THANKS FOR THE BAG.

ME: YOU'RE WELCOME.

KENT: IS YOUR MOM OKAY?

ME: SHE'S NOT DOING WELL. I'M GOING TO LOOK AFTER HER AND WE WILL COME VISIT TOMORROW. TELL JEN I SAID HI.

When he didn't respond immediately I tossed my phone into my purse. With the stereo as loud as it would go without deafening me, I drove home to my mother.

* * *

My puffy eyes strained to open the next morning as my phone chirped. I grabbed it and held it close to my face to get a good look.

Kent: Mom is awake.

I set the phone down and sighed. I was happy and at the same time dreading having to face him, especially if Jen were still by his side. I padded down the hallway and opened my mom's door. My mother was topless, her back to the door, and there was a man under her.

I screamed and turned tail and ran into my room, slamming the door. My heart felt like it was going to beat out of my chest. Jesus, I was glad she was getting out there but, why couldn't she have kept it under wraps while I was staying with her. I was picking things up off the floor to distract myself when a knock sounded at my door. "Elly, dear?"

"Mom, it's fine! I'm fine! I just... Kent's mom is awake, I thought you might want to know!" I yelled through the door, I couldn't face her right now either. Trauma all around the past couple of days; how tragic.

"Are you coming to the hospital with me?"

"Um... No, maybe you could take... Whoever was in your bed. I need to work this afternoon."

She paused for a moment and then said, "Alright. Make sure

you stop by tonight after your shift is over, Kent will appreciate it."

What did she know about what Kent would appreciate or not? Jen was probably still there, keeping him company, holding his hand, weaseling her way back into his life.

After I knew that my mom and her beau, who I had to admit was kind of a looker for an old man, were gone, I got into the waiting taxi and went to work.

It was busy, but it kept my mind off of everything that was going on. I checked my phone on my walk home, but there were no messages or missed calls waiting for me. I sighed, disappointed. And then I chastised myself for hoping that he was going to text or call me. He was off-limits, like always, and I had to get over it. I had to get over him. How the hell was I going to do that? I wasn't sure, but I was going to figure it out. I was going to start by avoiding him. Christmas was around the corner and the outlook was bleak at avoiding him during the upcoming holiday.

Chapter 28

I had just finished my shower when I heard my cellphone singing from my bedroom. I ran to catch it in time, taking a second to glance at the number before pushing the green button. Who in the world could be calling me from a New York phone number?

"Hello?" I said as I held my towel tightly to my chest.

"I'm trying to reach Backdrop." The man's voice was silky against the loud cacophony in the background. His words were clipped.

"Oh, um, yes. This is Elly. What can I do for you?" I asked.

"My name is Gavin and I'm with The Trumpeters. We had a corporate gig on Christmas Eve but we're stuck in this snow storm and can't get out of JFK. I googled some wedding bands and your name came up. Are you familiar with Derby and Associates?"

"Yes?..." That was Jen's father's medical group. What were the odds?

"Do you have a piece of paper? You need to write this down. Unless you already have a gig booked for that night?"

I quickly rushed over to my kitchen counter where the days mail was still sitting and snatched a pen from my junk drawer.

"Um, no. No gigs for Christmas Eve. Go ahead, I'm ready," I said as I squished the phone between my ear and shoulder and tried to hold my towel up with my under arms.

"You need to call Andy, he's Dr. Derby's assistant. You need to tell him that you are filling in for us and that you spoke with me, Gavin. I'd call him but I really fucking hate that guy. The set list was a bunch of soft pop hits and some jazzy Christmas crap. Probably anything will do. Just don't go too crazy. You dig?"

"Uh-huh." I quickly scribbled while he continued to spat directions at me.

"Dress is formal, very formal, like black tie and shit, and you need to arrive no later than three to set up and do your sound checks. Did I forget anything?"

"Um. Where is this party happening? The Hullendale Hotel or...?"

"It's at Northern University, in the York Building."

"Okay. Great. Well, thanks Gavin. I hope that--" The phone clicked in my ear before I got the rest out. Wow. I stared in surprise at the phone, half expecting he would call back and apologize for a dropped connection. I shook my head as I set it onto the counter beside my notes.

I stared. A gig, probably good paying, on Christmas Eve for a bunch of well dressed people. I smiled wide. I'd gotten my Christmas wish! I was going to be able to successfully dodge this Christmas Eve's festivities and, most of all, I'd get to dodge Kent!

I picked up my phone once the stunned stupor wore off and dialed Rio's number. "Rio? I have some great news!"

* * *

It felt weird returning to the university where I'd attended more than ten years ago. Oh the things I wish I could tell college Elly: Don't leave the dorm laundry room without your clean laundry in hand. Don't eat the salad bars on Wednesdays. Don't take Art History junior year. Don't go running to Kent every time you feel like you need a pick me up.

"Don't just stand there with your mouth hanging open, Elly, get the door! This drum is fucking heavy!"

James's voice cut through my daydreaming and I smiled. I wasn't in college anymore. I was an adult. And I had learned my lesson. Finally.

I opened the door wide so James could get his drum inside and held it while Rio and our new guitarist, Luke, followed after him. It hadn't been hard to replace Bryan after he was kicked from the band. I shuddered still to even think of him. What an asshole he'd been. But then, that was my type it seemed. I was doomed to be in relationships with asshole after asshole.

As we entered the Douglass Ballroom we were immersed in the pre-party set up. Crisp white tablecloths were being spread, sparkling Christmas-themed decorations were being hung, and the buffet tables were being prepared. I was glad that it wasn't me doing all the heavy lifting. As the singer I had it pretty easy as far as equipment went.

I was almost to the stage with my mic stand when I heard the voice of my nightmares.

"Elly Palmer! Is that you?"

I turned around and was face to face with Jen. She looked as beautiful as ever, not a hair out of place, even though she was in the middle of a flurry of people.

"Yep. It's me," I replied, trying to keep the venom from my voice.

"Well, what are you doing here?" she demanded, her body tilting to one side, all her weight pressing on the heel of a very expensive stiletto.

"My band is playing the party tonight."

She frowned and stared at her clipboard. She shook her head as her sapphire eyes met mine. "No, The Trumpeters are playing tonight."

I lightly scratched at an itch on my forehead as I stared at the back of her black clipboard. "No. They are trapped in a New York snow storm and asked us to fill in for them."

"Well does dadd--I mean, Dr. Derby know?"

I shrugged my shoulders and met her angry, confused eyes. "I don't know. I would assume so since I spoke with his assistant, Andy, this morning."

She sighed and rolled her eyes. "Alright. Fine. Go set up up there. You need to clear the stage by four and then start playing as guests arrive. Did you get the playlist?"

I nodded. It was a half truth.

She nodded in return and then smiled. "I tried to get Kent to come tonight but he said his mother needed him. I'll be sure to send my regards."

And just like that I wanted to punch her. My fists curled at my sides as my lips smiled. I had to put on the happy, work face.

"Yes, please do." I turned around and headed back to the stage. My Christmas Eve was looking slightly less appealing. I should have known that if her father was throwing an expensive party that Jen would be there.

Think of the money, Elly. And avoiding Kent. And the money.

I nodded to myself, strengthening my resolve. Yes. This was a good thing. And it was going to be a good night. There would be plenty of other people at this party and I'd find the hottest guy among them and sing to him all night long.

* * *

It turned out that Dr. Derby knew quite a few hot guys. I'd had my fill throughout the evening and only laid eyes on Jen once. She'd been at her dad's side, drowning herself in champagne. I guess the fall from her position as a housewife had gone into effect. She wasn't on Kent's arm anymore, now she was on her daddy's.

We were packing up to leave when a young man approached the stage. He cleared his throat, causing me to turn around and stare down at him.

"Yes?" I asked.

He held out a check in his hand. "Your payment for your services. Mr. Derby was quite pleased and made sure you were compensated well for the last minute changes."

I nodded and took the check. Etiquette kept me from staring at it until he'd turned away. When he did, I approached the guys and opened the envelope. I nearly fainted as I stared at the piece of paper which was shaking slightly in my hand.

"Holy shit," James exclaimed. He was always so eloquent.

"Elly, that can't be right. Go make sure he didn't write too many zeros," Rio insisted as he peered over James' shoulder.

I pulled it out further and glanced at the words written out.

Twelve thousand dollars and 00/100 ———

No, clearly it was not a typo. I glanced around at them and

smiled widely.

"Merry Christmas, you guys!"

"Merry Christmas!" James yelled as he pushed us all together and gave us a big squeeze. "I can rack up one helluva bar tab with three thousand smackers!" He fist pumped and then went back to quickly breaking down his drums.

Rio looked at me and smiled sadly. I turned away. I didn't need his pity. We'd just had a great night. I wasn't going to ruin it by thinking about him.

"You comin', Elly?" James asked as he turned his head in my direction.

"You bet," I said with a determined smile. I wasn't going to go home until I was mind-numbingly drunk.

Chapter 29

"I'll be really quick, thanks!" Stacy yelled as she dashed through my apartment towards the bathroom.

I watched her go but paused as my nose was accosted by something foul.

Sweet mother in heaven, what is that smell?

I wrinkled my nose and tried to sniff out the culprit. I walked towards the kitchen, the smell was gone. I walked back to the entryway. Definitely there somewhere. I ducked down and sniffed, moving closer and closer to the offending scent.

I grabbed a crumpled up sock and brought it to my nose.

"Oh god!" I turned my head away and held it out at arm's length.

"What is that?" Stacy asked as she came closer.

"A dirty sock," I said, holding it up for her to inspect.

She looked weirded out. "You should probably wash that."

"Thanks, smartypants. Did you smell it when you came in?"

She frowned as she came closer, her eyes inspecting me. "No. It's a dirty sock not a decaying body."

I pinched my nose and stared at her. "You can't smell that from there?"

She raised one eyebrow, a trick I'd always meant to learn but never had. "Um, no."

I quickly put the sock into the garbage and then washed my hands. "So what are you and Rio up to tonight?"

"Um... it's New Year's Eve, Elly. We're throwing a party. The one you're invited to and said you'd attend, remember?"

I dried my hands on the dishtowel and then came out to meet her questioning but hopeful eyes.

"Oh, right. Well, you better get out of here so I can get snazzied up," I said.

She grinned and pointed at me. "Yes! I'll see you later. Bring a date, if you want, maybe Kent."

I pointed back at her and shot her an imitation of a smile. "Maybe... not. It would be great if you could just not say his name. Thanks."

She rolled her eyes and waved me off as she headed for the front door. "Whatever, Elly. See you tonight!"

When she was gone I breathed a sigh of relief and lounged on my couch as I flipped on the TV. There was never anything good to watch on Saturday afternoons but as I began flipping I didn't really care. My eyes were so tired. I found Dirty Dancing and grabbed my throw blanket. Before the second commercial break I was fast asleep.

* * *

I woke up to the sound of Steve Carell yelling "MMOH -- KELLY CLARKSON!" I wiped the drool from the side of my mouth and sat up, glancing around to find the time. It was already a little past seven.

"Shit!" I leapt off the couch and ran towards the bathroom. I turned on the shower and while I was waiting for it to warm I grabbed my razor and studied it. It was too old so I tossed it and opened the cupboard beneath the bathroom sink. My tampons spilled out onto the floor and I grumbled to myself as I cleaned them up.

As I stuffed the last one into the box my mind niggled at me.

When was the last time I'd had my period? It should be coming soon.

I sighed and got up. It was just what I'd need: to start bleeding during the middle of a party. I jogged to my wall calendar and stared at it. I blinked a few times as I stared at the blank month. Where were the little red dots? Had I forgotten to mark it? No, I was very meticulous. I loved to have things written down, especially since I'd know exactly when the next one was coming. I flipped back to the previous month and started counting.

37.

37 days since my last period. I felt the color drain from my face as I stared at the calendar. Two pink dots a week before Christmas. Oh, God.

No.

I shook my head as I moved back to the shower and got in. Time and water were wasting.

I couldn't be pregnant. It was a fluke. It happened to everyone. I was probably just stressing out and my body was being difficult. I tried to hum it off, then sing it out of my mind but that didn't work. When I was out of the shower I quickly dressed in jeans and a sweatshirt, threw on my winter coat, and ran out the door. Nothing was going to put my mind at ease except a test. And I was very good at tests.

There was a pharmacy a few blocks down. I almost ran all the way there and on the way back I chugged a huge bottle of water. When I returned I took the test and set it on the sink. While the little test cooked itself I shaved because I'd forgotten to get my razor before getting in the shower. When I was done I closed my eyes and then grabbed the test. I'd made sure I'd gotten the digital kind. I didn't want to misread the thing.

I swallowed hard as I picked it up.

Please be negative, please be negative.

I opened my eyes and winced.

Pregnant

Damnit!

I threw the test into the trash but I couldn't tear my eyes away from the tiny word. Pregnant. I always used protection. Almost always. But when I didn't I got the morning after pill. I mentally calculated backwards and though I tried to resist I brought up the memory of my last dalliance.

Kent. On my bed. In the shower. Up against the wall. Getting dressed, missed phone calls. Hospital. Jen. Self-pity party. Lots and lots of waitressing.

Damnit!

I looked up and stared at myself in the mirror. It was too late to turn back now. I wasn't going to get rid of a baby. Did I go to Stacy's party and pretend everything was kosher? Or did I stay home and wallow in it? My whole life was about to change. Everything from my body to where I lived. My job. What was I going to do for money once the baby came? I couldn't go on singing. It wasn't practical. I'd be gone nights and weekends and I'd have to get a sitter and that wouldn't work out.

Kent.

No, I shook that thought away. I couldn't stick him with the baby every time I needed to work. That wouldn't be fair to him.

Yes it would! He's the father!

He's the father... Oh my God. I'd inadvertently pulled a Jen.

With shaking legs I moved to my bedroom and laid down. I pulled out my phone and sent a text to Stacy telling her that I was feeling sick. It was the truth. I was feeling very sick thinking about what the future was going to be like and the moment I was going to have to fess up and tell Kent that he was going to be a father.

I should've just texted him right then. I should've just ripped off the band-aid and gotten it over with. But I didn't. My fingers poised over the send key with the message I'd typed out to him.

--I'M PREGNANT. OOOPS.--

I quickly deleted it and set my phone down. That wasn't the right way to tell him. I'd wait until the next time I saw him. No, I'd wait until the second trimester. Lots of things could happen in the first trimester. Miscarriages were common, right? Like it had been with Jen?

I rolled over and curled up, a hand on my tummy. I didn't want it to end up like Jen. Not one bit of it. But my story was quickly becoming eerily similar.

Chapter 30

February

I removed the gloves from my hands and shoved them into my pockets as I smiled at the Asian woman standing behind the counter.

"Takeout or dine in?" she asked, her words hurried as I picked up and skimmed the paper menu.

"Um, take out... No, dine in," I quickly corrected myself and then started to unbutton my coat.

She nodded her acceptance of my final answer and then moved around the counter to show me to my seat.

As I rounded the corner I stripped off my coat and draped it over my arm. I glanced around a little, wondering if there was anyone there that I knew. There were some familiar faces from work but no one that I knew beyond what they liked to eat.

When the waiter came, I ordered two different dishes as well as two glasses of water. While I waited for the waiter to come back I absently put my hand on my stomach, which was not yet swollen.

I still hadn't said anything to anyone about the baby growing inside of me. I wasn't ready to face the fact that I was going to be a mother. I hadn't dreamed that this would happen to me – at least not this way. I was dreading the moment that I would have to tell the band that I was going to stop doing what I loved and be a responsible mother. But that's what I was going to do. And part of being a responsible mother was getting a responsible job. Tonight I was going to give my boss my two weeks notice and start seriously job hunting for something that was going to allow me to find a regular job with health insurance and benefits.

I heard laughing behind me which drew my attention away and as my eyes looked up they stuttered on someone entering the restaurant. Someone I hadn't seen in a couple of months. My vision was blocked when the waiter came and delivered my two plates of food.

I smiled and thanked him and then he moved away to check on another table.

My cheeks were on fire at the quick sighting of my ex-best friend. I was probably hallucinating like that time I thought I'd seen him walking down Center Street.

Despite what I might have feared, my ex-best friend wasn't with his renewed love interest Jen, but with a guy that appeared slightly older than him. I attempted not to stare as I tried to figure out who this mystery man could be. Did his mother have a new love interest as well? Was Kent on a job interview?

He was chatting with the other man until the hostess retrieved them and led them towards a table which happened to be behind where I was sitting.

When the pair moved by my table Kent's head turned to look at me. His double take was slightly amusing as he paused in his step, but I dared not to smile. Not as my heart was beating wildly, trying to escape from my chest in fear.

"Elly?" The confusion and disbelief clear in his voice as he stared at me as if I were a mirage.

His eyes didn't linger long. I half expected them to wander down over my stomach but they didn't because he had no way of knowing the secret I'd been hiding. Instead they moved over the empty seat and my table. Then his beautiful eyes looked away from me entirely.

No! His eyes weren't beautiful, they were roaming and deceitful.

Words flooded into my head along with emotions I didn't want to let out. This was not the place for it, not around these people, and certainly not in front of the stranger with him.

"Hey," I said, forcing a polite smile.

The stranger had paused as well and his eyes quickly assessed the situation. "I'll be at the table. I'll get a drink for you. No rush, Kent," he said and moved on, following behind the hostess who had paused when she saw her customers were distracted.

Kent stood there awkwardly for a moment as he pushed his hands into his pockets. "It's been awhile, Elly."

"Yeah... How is your mom?" I reached for my glass of water and sipped it as I craned my neck to stare up at him.

"She's getting along." His eyes were watching the guy he'd come in with, avoiding me completely. "How's yours?"

I swallowed hard but held the glass in my hand. "She's good." I nodded slowly trying to figure out what I was going to say next.

His eyes moved to me and then they moved to the empty seat across from me. I waited for him to say something. Anything.

His cheeks turned a bit pink as he shifted on his feet. "Well, I better go. Mom's nurse wanted to take me out because I've been cooking so much. Said I needed a break."

I nodded. It was all I could do. I glanced behind me towards the man, his mother's nurse, apparently, who was still waiting on Kent to sit down. He caught my eyes and offered me a smile. I managed to mirror him before turning back around.

"I should let you go on with your lunch," he said. And just like that Kent walked away from me and towards the table to where his acquaintance was sitting.

I felt the tears welling up so I kept my eyes bouncing around to try and prevent the impending meltdown. What had I been expecting? For him to just open up about how he'd resumed a relationship with Jen? He was many things but intentionally cruel wasn't one of them. I should've asked.

Actually, I should have gone with my first instinct and taken my food to go. I couldn't fix a lot of things but I could fix where I ate my lunch.

I cleared my throat, grabbed my things, and walked towards the cash register.

"Hi. I'm so sorry but I'm not feeling well. Can I have my food boxed to go?"

The hostess nodded as I pulled out my credit card and handed it to her. I made sure I wrote a generous tip and then waited for her to retrieve my food.

As I waited for the food I watched the nurse push the heavy front door open and not far behind him was Kent.

I stared and wrinkled my brow in confusion. Where the hell was he going? He'd just gotten here. Did the sight of me kill his appetite? My stupid tongue was still numb. I nodded like a dumbass and watched as he walked out. Kent never looked back as he pushed out the door and disappeared from view.

The food arrived in a plastic bag, pulling my attention away from the sudden departure. I grabbed it and headed out the door after bundling up. I sighed heavily as I turned and headed down the sidewalk towards my apartment. I don't know why I decided to look around me to see if I could find Kent. I guess it was still second nature no matter how much I tried to tell myself he was off limits.

He was standing at his car as he waved goodbye to the other man who left in a different car. He didn't look very happy.

I paused just for a second. I missed one step. And his eyes found mine.

Quickly I looked away. He'd written me off. Again. I needed to pay attention and read the signs and move on. So I resumed my walking.

I didn't get far before a pair of shoes were in front of me. My gaze moved up the muscular jean-clad legs. Why was he here? Hadn't he done enough to ignore me already? My gaze continued to take him in, slowly, I only made it halfway up his chest when he cut in.

"What's the matter? Your fuck buddy not show up?" I heard the anger in his words.

My eyes snapped to his as my heart started to beat furiously at his accusation. "Seriously?"

"I mean, shouldn't you send me a text to let me know you've moved on to the next guy, at least? Or is that not how the fuck buddy thing works?"

I shook my head at him in disbelief. I was speechless. Again. For one of the smartest men I'd known he was being utterly ridiculous.

He stood there with his hands curled in fists at his sides. I could feel his eyes burning me. If he could've sent me up in flames with just his gaze I would've been toast.

"First of all," I said, meeting his anger equally with my own, "I'm not fucking anyone—currently. Second of all, how dare you come over here and pretend to play the jealous boyfriend!"

He shook his head and looked away, as if I bored him. "Figures. Another jab at the fact that I wanted a relationship."

"You don't know what you fucking want, Kent! That's the problem! That's been our whole problem for our whole lives! Jen or Elly. Elly or Jen. Jen and a little Elly on the side — sure, that works. Marry Jen after fucking Elly. Fuck Elly and then fuck Jen. That works too."

His eyes had slowly come back to rest on me during my tirade. "Wow." He stood in front of me, his mouth open wide.

"Shut up. I'm sick of you! I'm sick of you and your fucking mind games!" I don't know what was coming over me or out of me. It just felt so good to get it out. "I'm done being convenient for you. I'm... I'm pregnant!"

"Great. Hope the father can deal with you and the kid."

My hand found its own mind and slapped him hard against his cheek. I shook out the tingles and the pain that resulted from it.

"It's your baby, you fucking asshole." I was surprised by how calm my voice was. Inside I was boiling.

Kent could barely contain his anger and for a second I wondered if I'd pushed him too far. And then it melted away as the color drained from his face. It was his turn to not have words for me.

"Don't worry. I'm not expecting some sort of proposal. I know how that turned out for you last time around." I was disappointed that my statement didn't hit its mark, and confused when his face continued to pale.

"You weren't going to tell me, were you?" His words came out of his lips in a whisper as his eyes went blank even as they searched my face. His head shook again.

I felt as if I'd been slapped. He really thought so little of me. "Go fuck yourself, Kent." I blinked back the tears that had been struggling to come out since I'd first seen him.

He looked as if he wanted to say something. I wanted him to so I could say more hurtful things. I wanted him to get angry with me, but instead his eyes lowered to the ground and he turned away from me. And he walked away. Like always.

Chapter 31

March

It had been three weeks since my run-in with Kent and I hadn't thought about him... much. Truth be told I was so busy with weddings and my new job search that I hadn't had much downtime to sit and agonize over what had happened between Kent and I.

Of course in the downtime I'd had I sat in front of the TV, watched sappy rom-coms and binged on ice cream. I was dreading stepping onto the scale today but I'd promised myself not to worry about it too much. I was even thinking about asking the nurse to not tell me the number. I didn't want to obsess. It wouldn't be healthy for myself or for the baby.

I was hustling to make it to my doctor's appointment and I was so self-involved that I didn't see the hand dart out in front of me and grab the handle. My hand touched the masculine one on the door and sparks moved through my body. I glanced up and it was him! As if burned, I jumped back and crossed my arms over my chest, which had been growing at an alarming rate.

"What are you doing here?" I demanded, meeting his gaze, making sure he could see plainly how very little I wanted to see him.

He swung open the door and stood aside so that I could go in. When I looked towards the open door his other hand touched the small of my back, ushering me inside.

I clenched my jaw. He probably thought that I wouldn't cause a scene in my doctor's office. I smiled to myself as I went to the desk and checked in. Once that was done I ignored him and went to an empty seat between two pregnant women and pulled out my cellphone.

I didn't dare glance up from it because I could feel his eyes on me as he sat across the aisle. I saw with my peripherals that his feet were crossed at the ankles and his hands were folded together in front of his crotch. I wondered how uncomfortable he was. I hoped it was off the charts.

The nurse came out and called two names. Neither were mine. The two women on either side of me got up and headed towards the nurse and upon seeing the open space Kent quickly jumped into it.

"I'm here for your doctor's appointment. Your mom told my mom that I'd probably want to come."

I rolled my eyes and kept them focused on the webpage I was scrolling through slowly, as if reading it.

"You're not coming in there with me. You can leave now," I said, not bothering to hide the disinterest in my voice.

"Elly, come on. This is my baby too and I should be allowed to be involved," he retorted, bending forward to try to get my attention.

"You will be. Once it's born. Until then there isn't anything for you to do." I kept my eyes down, continuing to ignore him.

"I can help you with lots of stuff. Stress is bad for the baby and I'm sure it's stressful in your life with the band and work and stuff."

I turned my eyes to him, finally. He looked hopeful. I was going to shut that down real fast.

"The only stress in my life is you. If you want to de-stress me then you should leave. I don't want to see you."

He studied my face and his hopeful expression fell. I turned my attention back to my phone, the feeling of accomplishment swelled in my chest. Finally I was able to tell Kent off and ignore him and shut him down for once. It felt good.

"Is that really how you feel or are you just angry about what I said?" he asked.

"Which part are you talking about? The part where you called me a loose woman or the part where you called me an inconsiderate bitch?"

I heard a sharp inhale of his breath.

"I didn't call you either of those things."

"You implied them. It's the same thing."

"Elly. Christ. Come on. You're putting words into my mouth. I was surprised."

"Yeah, well. I'm sure you didn't say those things to Jen when she broke her news to you. You fell to your knees and offered her your life. So... yeah. Fuck off."

He was so quiet and so still beside me that I snuck a glance. His jaw was twitching angrily beneath red cheeks, his eyes turned away. I felt the smile come upon my lips. Finally, I'd struck him where it hurt.

The nurse opened the door and called my name. I stuffed my phone into my purse after putting it on silent and then got up, heading for her. She smiled at me, which I returned, and then her eyes fell behind me and she offered another smile. I stopped and turned around, pointing at him.

"I already told you, you can't come to my appointment, Kent. Go home!"

He flashed his charming smile at the nurse. "I was just hoping I could listen to the heartbeat today. The doctor will be checking that, won't she?"

The nurse nodded as she glanced between us. She seemed unaffected and it left me wondering how often she saw this sort of thing.

"I can call you in when it's time, if that's okay with Ms. Palmer." The nurse's eye came to rest on me and suddenly I felt like a jerk. They were ganging up on me.

I rolled my eyes. "Fine."

The part where my stomach was exposed and the gel was squirted onto it came too quickly. I looked away from Kent, focusing instead on the doctor who gently pressed the wand to my stomach. In a matter of seconds the fast, rhythmic whooshing of our baby's heart was echoing throughout the room. The doctor let us listen for a minute and then smiled.

"A nice steady 173. The baby sounds great."

The doctor put a wad of paper towels in my hand as she cleaned up her tool. I moved to clean it only to have the paper towels taken from me. Kent wiped off my stomach with care reserved for a baby with a sore bottom. I frowned at him but he ignored me.

"So, if we had one of those machines we could listen to the baby's heart rate anytime we wanted to?"

The doctor nodded with a smile, "Oh yes. And they aren't terribly expensive."

He nodded as he moved over to throw the paper towels away. I pulled my shirt down and sat up, I was almost there when I felt Kent's hand on my back, helping me the rest of the way. I clenched my jaw tightly to keep my angry retort inside.

The doctor's eyes looked between us and then down to a pad of paper she had on the desk. She scribbled something and then held it out to Kent.

"Here is a list of the best ones on the market."

She looked down again and started scribbling something else and then held it out to me.

"And here is the brand of stool softener I recommend. The constipation is only going to get worse, especially if we have to supplement your iron."

I took the paper with pink cheeks and held it on my lap.

"Thanks."

"So, I'll see you again in a few weeks if your blood test is normal. We'll draw today and if anything is amiss we will give you a call. Nurse Thomas will help you at the end of the hall, just let her know you need your first trimester test."

I nodded again. Already I felt my anxiety sky-rocketing. Blood test. Blood. I exhaled deeply as I tried to hold myself together.

After she left the room I pushed myself off the table and put my shoes back on. Luckily I hadn't been in one of those paper gowns. I shoved the doctor's paper into my purse and then opened the door and peeked down the hallway. The chair was there in plain sight. It was brown and ugly. Empty viles waiting to capture fresh blood were sitting just to the left of the table.

"I'll hold your hand, if you want." Kent's voice was gentle and comforting at my back.

Oh, how I wanted him to hold my hand. But this was one of those things, one of many, that I was going to have to get used to doing on my own.

"Nope. I'm good. You heard the baby, you can go now. Bye." I forced my feet to carry me towards the torture I was about to endure. I also forced myself not to look back.

Once Nurse Thomas seated me I got to see him anyway. He was walking towards the exit, his hands shoved deep into his pockets, his shoulders drooping. I felt the pinch in my arm and closed my eyes tightly.

Be strong, Elly, for the baby. Don't look.

Chapter 32

My mother had been begging since New Year's for me to come over and see her. Partly I think she wanted to see if I'd blown up like a balloon, which I hadn't. And the other part was to, I think, get me to formally meet the man she'd been seeing. His name was Colin and he greeted me at the front door after I'd rung the bell.

"Elly! How lovely to see you. Please, come in. Your mom is in the kitchen."

I peeled my coat from my shoulders and handed it over to the man who was smiling at me as if he'd just met his long-lost daughter. It was weird.

I smiled nervously. "Thanks." I watched as he put my coat onto a hanger and then turned back towards me. I raised my eyebrows but he didn't make a move to introduce himself. "I'm sorry. Colin, right?"

He laughed and held out his hand. "Oh, forgive me. I've heard so much about you that I feel like we are old friends. Colin, yes, Colin Struthers. It's a pleasure, Elly. I hope you don't mind my being here."

I smiled as I shook his hand. "You're clothed, so I'm good."

Both of our cheeks turned a light shade of pink.

"I'm so sorry about that. It won't happen again," he insisted.

I nodded uncomfortably and then pointed over his shoulder towards the kitchen. "So my mom is in there?"

"Yeah, yeah! Go ahead, I was just going to put some music on when I heard the doorbell."

"Okay. Well, I'll see you in there."

He nodded and chuckled and then set off for the living room as I diverted myself towards the kitchen. My mom had really outdone herself. There were pies and cookies covering the island's surface. She was pulling a lasagna from the oven and a large salad was in a serving bowl by the sink.

"Wow. This is a lot of food for just the three of us. I finally met Colin, formally, you know. He seems... nice."

My mom turned around as soon as she heard my voice and closed the distance between us, giving me a huge hug after setting down her lasagna. "He is nice. Very nice." She pulled away and her eyes dropped down to my stomach which was only slightly puffed out. It looked like I'd eaten too much food. "How are you doing?" she asked, her eyes meeting mine again.

I smiled as I leaned against the counter. "I'm just fine."

"Are you eating enough at home? I remember when I was pregnant with you I couldn't keep anything down."

"Yeah, not really my problem. I have a super-human nose." I also had boobs that felt like they were constantly in a vice but I wasn't going to talk about that just before dinner. I didn't want my mom to lose her appetite.

"Hmm. Well how was the doctor's visit?"

"Mmm. Yeah, it was okay. Until Kent showed up."

She turned away from me to take plates down from the cupboard. "Oh? It's good that he wants to be involved."

"I guess. But if I'd wanted him at the appointment I would have told him about it myself. You can't do that, Mom, or I'm going to stop telling you things."

She turned around to give me the mom eye. It sent shivers through me.

"Elly. Listen to me. Kent isn't going to keep chasing after you forever. Your baby needs a father in his or her life and it's your responsibility to make sure he or she gets one."

I frowned at her. I knew he wasn't going to keep chasing after me forever. I was banking on that fact. He was going to get bored and move on to the next conquest once he realized I wasn't what he wanted. And I didn't want my heart getting broken again in that process. "I didn't have a father in my life and I turned out just fine." Once I'd said it I knew I shouldn't have but it was too late to take it back.

My mother's lips pressed together in a thin line and then her eyes started to water.

I looked away and blinked back my own tears. Damnit. This contagious emotions thing was getting out of control.

"Elly. I want something better for you. You have no idea how hard it was to raise you by myself. And you are so lucky to have a man that wants to stick around and be a father. I don't want to see you blow it."

"Mom." I pressed at the corners of my eyes to keep the tears at bay. "I love you but you don't know everything. Do you want me to marry a guy just because he happened to get me pregnant?"

"No, but Kent isn't just any guy."

"No, you're right. He's the guy that I loved. But that's past tense. It's gone now. I won't ever be enough for him and I realize that now and it's best that I see it now before I give in and say yes and get my heart broken all over again."

She held the plates out to me, a sad ghost of a smile on her lips. "I won't say another thing about it. But..."

"But what?" I asked with a sigh.

"You're going to have to see him again."

I rolled my eyes as I took the plates from her and turned

towards the dining room. "I know. He'll get joint custody of the ba–"

I stopped as I stared straight ahead of me. He was standing there in the doorway of the kitchen. How much had he heard? I lifted my chin. It didn't matter. I hadn't said anything that he didn't already know. Except that maybe he should just give up now. He was wasting his breath trying to get me to be anything other than his baby's mama. There was no changing that.

"Hi, Elly. Can I take those for you?" He held his hands out for the plates.

I held them tighter against my chest which almost caused me to wince. "No, thanks, I've got them."

As I moved into the dining room I heard him chatting casually with my mother. And as I set the table I heard more voices in the living room. Kent's mom and Colin and someone else I didn't recognize were talking politics. When I was done eavesdropping I stepped back and bumped right into Kent.

The tingles and the heat that moved through me were so unfair and while I tried to jump away from him, his hands were firmly planted on my hips, to steady me or to hold me there, I wasn't sure.

I cleared my throat and raised my eyebrows. He stared down at me. His eyes were melting my resistance. I looked away and stepped back.

"You shouldn't sneak up on people like that."

"I beg to differ," he said, his voice incredibly thick and sexy.

I cleared my throat again before the lust choked me. This was going to be a challenge. I had never before had to beat Kent off with a stick. Not for any real amount of time and certainly not over weeks and weeks when my body was screaming out for his touch!

He stepped closer, not letting distance come between us.

"Elly, I've been thinking about what happened between us and what was said." I wanted to interject but I was too curious. "I was burning up with jealousy thinking that you might be with someone else. And I know that's crazy. You deserve better than an asshat like myself. You deserve..."

My nails were biting into my curled fists. I was bursting to speak, to make him stop but I didn't have to because my mother did it for me.

"Can you two tell the others that dinner is ready?"

I glanced over Kent's shoulder and nodded, forcing a smile. I saw the look of confusion and then dismay on her face when she realized she'd interrupted a moment between us. It was for the best. It was best if there was nothing between us. I knew how it would end. Heartbreak. There was no other way between Kent and I.

I left the room briefly and returned with the other guests at my back. I tried to back away when I saw Kent down on his knee but there was nowhere to run. I was surrounded by people. There was a gasp that I recognized to be my mother's.

I shook my head at Kent, begging him silently not to do this because I already knew the answer.

"Elly. I know that you deserve better than me. And I know that the circumstances make it hard for you to see what this really is. I don't want to marry you just because you're carrying my child. I want to marry you because I love you. I have had these feelings for a long time. We both know that. I was unfair to Jen. I was unfair to you. And I'm so sorry. I want to spend my lifetime trying to make it up to you. I want you to make me a better man. I want to be the man you deserve. Please, Elly. Will you marry me?"

He lifted a light blue box that was the signature of the famous New York jeweler and then opened it to reveal a dazzling diamond engagement ring. The center stone surrounded by tiny pink stones which were also surrounded by more diamonds.

Again I tried to take a step back. This wasn't happening. It was probably one of those weird pregnancy dreams I'd read about. But those usually had lots of sex in them. Oh god. What was he doing? Kent's mom's warm hand rested on my shoulder, forcing me to confront him and everyone else in the room instead of fleeing.

"Why did you do this? You know the answer," I said, my throat thick with emotions that I didn't want to confront.

I saw his jaw twitching under his taut skin. "Tell me."

I paused, watching him, did he really want me to do this?

"No, I will not marry you. You say it's not because of the baby but it is. You want to do the right thing but the right thing isn't marrying the girl who you feel lukewarm for, Kent. I won't ruin your life the way Jen did."

"Elly!–"

It was all I heard him say before I turned around and pushed through my mother's guests. I had to get out of there. I wasn't about to have dinner and have everyone staring at me. I grabbed my coat and Kent's keys and rushed out the door.

Before I knew the destination I turned the keys in the ignition and pulled out of the driveway.

Chapter 33

I was livid, burning livid, that Kent had dared to humiliate both of us that way. A proposal in front of family? Was he thinking I would say yes due to peer pressure. Did he even know me at all? I was seriously beginning to wonder.

I was driving, to where I wasn't sure. I was hungry, my stomach grumbled reminding me that I hadn't eaten anything since early this morning. In ten minutes I was parked in front of Tony's with only one thing on my mind – carbs.

As I got out and headed to the door I pulled out my phone and called Stacy. I needed to vent and I needed someone semi-neutral. So I went with the natural choice.

"Hey, Elly. What's up?" she asked. I heard the faint sound of a TV in the background and lots of rustling.

"Hey. Are you with Rio?"

She scoffed, pretending to be offended. "Why would you assume that I'm with him?"

"Don't answer a question with a question, Stacy. I need to talk," I said.

"What am I? Chopped liver?"

"No. I need both of you. Can you guys meet me at Tony's as

soon as possible?" I asked, my voice wobbling because I was close to losing it.

"The one in town or the one by the hardware store?"

"In town."

"Alright. We'll be there," she said before hanging up the phone.

When they entered together twenty minutes later I almost felt bad. It was obvious from the state of their faces and their hair that they had been in the middle of something when I'd called, or at least at the very end of it.

The pizza arrived when they did and as the hot pie sat between us all I inhaled deeply. If heaven had a smell I was sure that pizza was it. When I opened my eyes they were both staring at me. Rio had one of his eyebrows raised. Both of Stacy's eyebrows were almost touching her hairline.

"What?" I said as I looked between them.

"You were just sniffing the pizza. Like nose to cheese," Stacy said quietly.

I frowned as I wiped at my nose. It wasn't wet with grease and I hadn't burned it.

"No, I was not!"

Rio cleared his throat and looked away as Stacy shrugged her shoulders. Whatever weirdness I'd exhibited had apparently been forgiven. That's how you knew people were your true friends.

"So is this about Kent?" Stacy was the first to start the conversation as she handed out the plates that had been placed on the edge of the table.

I sighed deeply.

"Right. What did he do this time? Stick his tongue down Jen's throat while you were looking?" Stacy lifted a slice but quickly set it back down once her brain registered the too hot temperature.

"No. He proposed."

They both looked like frozen versions of themselves but Stacy cracked first.

"Elly! Oh my god! That's so great!" She'd grabbed onto Rio's leather jacket and tugged it. His body moved with the force but he was still frozen. Then she reached across the table and snatched my left hand. She frowned at the lack of carats. "Where is it? I want to see it!" She gasped and let go of my hand. Her voice dropped to a whisper. "Are you keeping it a secret?"

Rio finally woke up. He leaned into Stacy's side and spoke into her hair. "Let her talk, baby." Once she nodded and closed her lips he sat back and met my eyes. He nodded, giving me the floor.

"I told him no," I said.

Again, I was met with statues. I sighed and frowned.

"Come on, guys! Kent! Proposing! That's so messed up on so many levels. He's only doing it because I'm pregnant. And how can I accept a proposal based on that? He's had years and years to make his move and he didn't until he finally realized that Jen wasn't the right woman for him. And then he rebounded with me and knocked me up and now he's going through the motions and lining himself up to be very unhappy for the second marriage of his life? No. I don't think so. I mean, you guys agree, right? I'm not crazy."

Stacy and Rio looked at each other. Some unspoken language passed between their tense bodies before she turned her eyes back to me.

"Elly. I've known you for many years now–"

"Arg!" I cut her off and shook my head as I grabbed a slice. "Forget it. I don't understand why no one understands!" Suddenly and without warning my anger turned into sadness and tears blinded me. The pizza that was in my grasp was now just a blur of beige and orange.

"Hey," Rio purred as he took a seat next to me and wrapped his arm around my shoulder. "We are here to support you. If you don't want to marry that guy, then don't. We aren't on his team, Elly. We are on yours. We just want you to be happy. No more tears. It's going to be alright."

I tried to let his words soak in as he held me against his warm, comforting chest. Stacy was so lucky to have caught a man like Rio. But I know it hadn't been easy to do. Why did love have to be so hard?

Why did we have to love anyone at all?

I sighed as I put my hand to my stomach. Perhaps love wasn't such a bad thing. No matter what happened I knew I was going to love this person growing inside of me.

* * *

After pizza and girl talk I called Kent's cellphone. I'd stolen his car in my haste to disappear. He picked up almost immediately.

"Are you alright?" he asked.

I swallowed back my retort, which would have been less than nice.

"Yes. Your car is at Tony's. I'm leaving the keys with the manager. I told him to make sure he carded you for confirmation of your identity."

"Elly–"

"I have to go. Bye." I hung up the phone before he had the opportunity to sweet talk me and try to change my mind or make me more upset than I already was. He was going to make a mistake if he married me, I knew he would. And I deserved better than a post-pregnancy marriage proposal. I deserved a man who wanted me for me.

Rio and Stacy dropped me off at my apartment and I made a bee-line for my bed. I was so tired. The days events had exhausted me and my belly was full of carbs. Yummy, yummy carbs. I plopped down onto the bed, my arms stretched out wide. I yawned and curled onto my side. I opened my eyes and stared at my hand resting on the pillow beside me. It was Kent's pillow. A few months ago he was laying there. For the first and last time.

Chapter 34

I was still dressed in my work clothes when I came into the doctor's office. I checked in and sat down with a huff. My feet were killing me and I was so, so tired.

It had been a month since my last appointment and I was eager to hear the baby's heartbeat again.

I'd texted Kent about the appointment and was slightly disappointed that he wasn't there. I chided myself for feeling that way. And angry at myself for letting him get to me. This was exactly why I didn't want to get married to him. I didn't want to feel disappointed when he wasn't there for me.

I picked at a ball of fuzz that was on my leggings. Super comfortable and I could wear most of my old dresses without fear of bending over and showing everyone my pregnancy panties. The dresses were the most uncomfortable in the chest.

He should have been there for my anyway, my thoughts wandered, as a friend if nothing else. Why couldn't we just raise this baby together as friends? I glanced up when the nurse came out but she called another name. I let out a sigh of slight impatience. If I wasn't waiting for anyone else to come I at least wanted to go in there and get this over with.

I tried to imagine my future. I'd be living in a tiny little house with a backyard that was big enough for my baby to play in. Maybe I'd get one close to Rio so that he could help out if I needed him to. I'd run around the neighborhood pushing the baby in the stroller to try to keep up my looks. I'd meet someone. I'd go on dates but constantly be checking my phone, worrying about the baby. Kent would text me 500 times about the baby. No, he'd be across the restaurant with another woman. Enjoying himself. Care free.

I looked towards the door as it opened and my heart stuttered in my chest. Kent was rushing inside, his eyes frantically looking around the waiting room until they landed on me. I was waiting for his comforting smile but it never came. He was frowning as he made his way over.

"Sorry I'm late. Mom's nurse quit so I've been interviewing all morning and I hit every red light on the way here." He looked like he was going to reach out for my hand but it went to his hair instead, his fingers gliding through it to try to ease his frustration.

I cleared my throat and smoothed down my skirt, trying to pretend as if I weren't burning up with jealousy at the mere thought of him having dinner with another woman.

"It's fine. You made it," I said, pulling my gaze from his. I felt my nipples tightening beneath my bra. The nearness of him was getting me all riled up. I glanced down at my stomach and wondered if I were too pregnant for a casual encounter. The horniness raging in my body was getting to be too much. Maybe I'd swing by the porn shop on the way home and grab something nice to play with.

I jumped in surprise as I felt Kent's warmth breath on my ear. "You look beautiful today," he said, his voice all husky.

I frowned at him but before I could say anything the nurse came out and called for me. We stood up together, I was now flustered thanks to his comment and I hoped no one else would be able to smell my excitement, least of all him. I went through the motions, answered the questions, kicked Kent out when it was time to check my weight. I still didn't know how much I'd gained, if anything. It was a sore subject for me.

Kent stayed quiet throughout the whole of the appointment. He didn't say anything when it was time to hear the baby, he just stood beside me, his eyes alternating between my stomach and the doctor.

I was growing increasingly irritated as the appointment was wrapping up.

"Did you purchase one of the monitors?" the doctor asked, her attractive face smiling at Kent.

"Uh, no," he said. He opened his mouth to say more and then shut it, his cheeks going pink.

I rolled my eyes as I cleaned off my stomach. This was disgusting. And how dare they flirt right in front of me.

"Elly is going to be having lots of changes before the next time she comes in for an appointment. If you're going to get one, I suggest you do it soon," the doctor said, "Did you misplace the paper that I gave you?" Was she looking at him with hope in her eyes?

"No, I've still got it." Kent smiled and then scratched the back of his head. "What kind of changes will she be going through?"

The doctor grinned. "You should get a book called 'What to Expect When You're Expecting;' its pretty much the industry standard. It will outline everything that she'll be going through in great detail."

Kent nodded, taking in the information.

"But the short answer is that she'll begin to show as the baby continues to grow. She might even feel the baby start to move. And at the next appointment we will schedule your ultrasound so we can determine the sex of the baby."

Kent blinked, stunned. I watched as his face turned from interest to awe.

I cleared my throat as I sat up and pulled my dress down to my knees. He offered his hand as I slid towards the edge of the patient chair. I took it and smiled at the doctor.

"We'll head to the bookstore right after this appointment. Unless Kent has other things to do." I turned my eyes to meet his and he shook his head. I nodded and then looked back to the doctor with a smile, stepping closer to Kent, silently marking my territory. She couldn't try to dig her claws in him until I was at least delivered. How awkward would that be to have your OB dating the father of your child?

"Did you come by taxi?" Kent asked as we walked out of the doctor's office.

"Yeah."

"I'll give you a ride then, to the bookstore." His smile was back, basking me in its warmth.

"Sure," I said as my feet carried me towards the parking lot. I didn't want him getting the wrong idea. This wasn't a date and I wasn't going to get moony-eyed over him.

We rode to the bookstore in silence, letting the radio give us an excuse not to speak. It was awkward, a little weird and familiar all at the same time.

"I don't think we've ever been to a bookstore together," I said as we approached the store.

He held the door open for me with a grin. "Yeah. Some of us like to read more than others."

I hit him with my knuckles in the middle of his chest as I walked past him. "Shut up. I was busy with other things."

"Oh, I know. Chatting online with boys was your favorite extra-curricular activity."

"Ha. That's just what I led you to believe. Doing things to try to get you to notice that I was a girl was my favorite extra-curricular activity."

His face fell, the merriment from a moment ago gone. I ignored it and pointed towards the back, hoping it was the right way. "Over here, I think."

He followed behind me in silence as I made my way towards the parent section of the bookstore. I stood back, my eyes wide as they roamed over the various titles on display. There were so many.

"Ah. Here it is," he said as he plucked the thick book from the shelf. There were at least twenty identical ones still on the shelf.

I let my eyes wander and smiled as they landed on a title that spoke to me. 'Pregnant Sucks.' I picked it up and turned to the table of contents. My finger skimmed down the page slowly. I tapped

"Your Superhero Nose" and closed the book. This was it. The winner.

"Whatcha got there?" Kent asked, trying to reach for my book. I twisted away, holding it firmly under my arm.

"None of your business."

"Oh. Sorry." He looked around the bookstore and then at me. "Did you want to shop for anything else while we're here?"

"Nope. You?"

He shook his head and then opened his hand in the direction of the registers. "After you, Miss."

I rolled my eyes.

We got back into his SUV, a grin on his lips because he'd won the payment debate that was going on in front of the cashier. He set the books on the floor beside my feet and went about driving towards my apartment.

I tried to ignore it but it was hard not to. "You may have won that battle but you are far from winning the war, my friend."

He glanced at me, one eyebrow raised. "Oh? We are friends again?"

I shrugged and pretended to stare out the window. "We should be. If we're going to raise the baby together."

"Together?" There was a hint of optimism in his voice. I turned to look and an even bigger ray of hope was shimmering from his expressive eyes.

"Not together, together. Together as in co-parents."

"So how is this going to work exactly? Will the baby live with me part of the week and live with you part of the week? Or will I get to look after him when you go to work at night and you'll look after him during the day? Because I'm not sure how well that will work since you'll be exhausted when you come by to pick him up. And we wouldn't want to wake him up in the middle of his REM cycle. And–"

"Kent!" I put my hands on my forehead, trying to press all of his mouth vomit from my mind. "I just... I haven't figured it out yet. I'm still trying to figure out if I want an epidural or a natural birth. Besides you don't know what's going to happen in the next few months. There might be someone else in our lives."

"You mean your life? Are you seeing someone?" His knuckles turned white as he gripped the steering wheel tighter. His jaw was twitching angrily.

"Kent."

His eyes turned to me and his expression softened a little. "I'm sorry," he cleared his throat before he continued, "I'm sorry. I just... I'll learn how to deal with that stuff. But it's going to take time and it's not going to be easy. I just want you to know that. It isn't going to change."

I reached down and pulled 'Pregnancy Sucks' from the shopping bag and settled it on my lap. "You aren't a psychic. You never know what might happen."

"I know that I'm not ever going to stop loving you, Elly. And I know that I'm never going to stop waiting for you. No one else is going to share my bed, my heart. Except our child. He'll have a special place there, but a different one."

I shook my head, anger rising in my chest at his ridiculous sentiments. Probably all lies. I needed to change the subject. "How do you know it's going to be a boy?"

He grinned. "I just know it."

Chapter 35

"Elly, we need to talk."

I stared at his foot in my doorway for a long moment before meeting his determined eyes.

"I have nothing to say to you."

"Maybe you think you don't but I think you do. You used to tell me everything. You used to talk to me about guys. And you used to talk to me about everything that was bothering you. Like when Billy kept crowding you in line when we were in third grade. Or that time Tanya called you retarded because you couldn't kick the soccer ball. You used to share everything with me, Elly. And I want you to share with me again."

"Well, those times are over. We haven't shared everything since fifth grade. Because in sixth grade I fell for you. I've had a crush on you since then and I've been lying to you ever since. Because how could I tell you that I liked you? You would have blushed and walked the other way."

His large hand gripped the edge of my door and forcefully pushed it open, letting himself in. I retreated until my knees hit the back of the couch.

"Elly, you have no idea what I would have done. And you're right. We haven't been honest with each other. Do you remember that first day, in eighth grade, when you came to school dressed in those torn jeans? And you had a flannel shirt on and you'd just dyed your hair magenta?"

I nodded though I wish I could have blocked out that day. Everyone stared at me. Girls in class were whispering and giggling.

The guys chuckled and made rude comments.

"You held your head up high even though you were being picked on. I realized my crush on you that day. But I couldn't tell you. You were coming out as the cool outcast and I was still the class nerd. I wasn't good enough for you. I never have been. I kept waiting for you to meet the guy who was going to sweep you away from me. The cool outcast guy who had his ear pierced or something."

I rolled my eyes, this was getting ridiculous.

He sighed heavily as he ran his hands roughly through his hair.

"Just tell me the truth. Tell me what's been going on inside your head. I need to understand because I know that when you tell me that you won't marry me that it's a lie. Because every time I'm around you I feel whole. And I can't go around the rest of my life feeling half empty inside."

"Do you want to know the truth? I think you're only here and trying so hard because I'm pregnant," I said.

He blew a puff of exasperated air through his nose.

"Elly. Have I ever lied to you?"

I didn't even hesitate. "Yes."

He closed his eyes in frustration. "Okay, yes, fine. That was a dumb question. When I lied to you, why was I lying?"

"Because you're a dick?"

"No. I lied because I didn't want to get hurt. But it never worked out and in the process I hurt you. I was a dumbass. But I'm done with that. Pregnant or not pregnant, I love you. Pregnant or not pregnant, I want to be with you. I wish I believed that you don't feel that way for me but I know that's not true. You love me too. You desire and crave me just as much as I desire and crave you."

And now it was time to face my fears and just be blunt and ask him the question I'd been dying to know the answer to since high school. "Did you love Jen?"

He paused for a long moment, his gaze flickered to the side of me and I watched as he processed his life for the past fifteen years.

"At first I thought I did. I loved things about her. I loved that she was so confident and she could fit into any social situation and how she could make friends so easily. She made it really easy for me to say yes to her. For the most part. She knew how to manipulate me." His eyes met mine, his tone final. "I convinced myself that I did love her. But no, I didn't."

"Then why did you marry her?"

"Because I wasn't good enough for the woman I really wanted."

"But you are now?"

His eyes met mine and he stared. His gaze melting me it was so intense. "No. I'm not. But I'm hoping that you'll take me anyway because I'm done hurting you. I'm done denying myself. Life is too short. And too precious. Mom told me that."

I was quiet. My mind was racing. His words were jumbling in my subconscious. He waited. He waited as I stood there and shuffled from one foot to the other. Did I accept what he'd said? Did I accept that he wanted to be with me for the right reasons?

"I can't promise to marry you, Kent."

His face and shoulders fell, his eyes fell to the floor and he nodded once. "Okay. Well, at least I tried." He chewed on the inside of his cheek as his eyes lowered to his hand which was fishing something from his pocket. He withdrew the ring box and held it out to me, closed. "When you believe that I love you then you can leave this somewhere for me to find and I'll know that I'm finally worthy of you, Elly."

He came forward and pressed a soft kiss to my lips, which were trembling. This felt an awful lot like goodbye. I put my hand to his chest when he pulled away. He smiled softly at me and took a step backwards and then another until his hand was on the doorknob.

When he was through the door I glanced at the ring box in my hand and then looked at my other one. My fingertips were bloodied.

"Kent! You're blee–" My vision started to darken and I wobbled.

No, no, no. This wasn't going to happen. I grabbed onto the doorframe tightly and closed my eyes. I heard footsteps rushing back as I felt myself losing my grip on the door.

"Woah, Elly."

Strong hands grabbed me and then I was weightless and floating.

"I've got you," he said. His voice was so soothing. "Are you still with me?"

"Mhm."

"Do I need to take you to the hospital?"

I tried to think of something, anything, to distract me but all I could see was his blood on my fingertips. My soft couch was on my back now, supporting me and I felt his warmth move away. "You're bleeding."

"I'm no–" His voice cut off as clothing rustled. "Damnit. I am." His warmth returned by my side but I didn't dare open my eyes.

"Is it bad? What happened?"

"Oh, you know, the usual. I got into a tangle at the bar with a half man, half shark."

Suddenly that image was in my head and my eyes popped open at the absurdity of it. I was rewarded with his warm, sexy smile. His hand moved to my forehead and smoothed it back. It was comforting. His hand came back again and his thumb traced the line of my lower lip. It trembled against his touch.

How was he able to make me go from sickly to confused to turned on so quickly?

"I'm okay. I got a tattoo. But I promise I'm okay."

He moved his hands to mine and gave them a squeeze.

I was even more confused. "Of what?"

He got up and moved away, towards the kitchen. I heard some running water and then he was back, a wet paper towel in his hand. He didn't say anything, he just cleaned off my fingers. And I let him and put my head back onto the couch pillow.

"I'd show you, Elly, but you'd just pass out."

"I don't care. Show me anyway."

He stared at me, his eyes moving over my face. I could see the internal struggle going on in his mind. "Alright." He unbuttoned his shirt slowly and before I could twist it into something sexy I saw the top of the bandage. I blinked, trying to hold it together as the blood came into view. I closed my eyes as he took the side of it and pulled it down. A few seconds later he said, "Alright, you can look now."

I opened my eyes and stared.

Like a brand it was there, my name on his chest. And just like a fresh brand it was angry around the edges, angry and red. He allowed to look for a minute before buttoning up his shirt. His hand was holding the dangling bloodied bandage and it was flapping around like a flag. It was the last thing I saw before everything went black.

Chapter 36

I didn't know how long I'd been passed out for but when I woke up I was alone. I laid there for awhile, letting everything come back to me. My talk with Kent. The ring. The tattoo.

I glanced at the front door. It was still closed and my mind was left wandering. Maybe I'd been dreaming or delirious. Maybe he hadn't come by at all. My eyes fell to the little light blue box that had been carelessly dropped on the floor. I wondered if I should open it. Inside was a promise. A promise to marry Kent. To be his wife. To be his for as long as we could both stand each other.

I nibbled my lower lip and went over, opening the box. The ring inside was still as fresh and sparkly as it had been the other night when he'd whipped it out before dinner. It was beautiful. And so very me. My fingers inched towards it slowly. I hesitated. Should I touch it? I didn't want to get it dirty. What if I was never ready? Was he going to let me hold onto it forever? It would be a punishment to know that I held such a thing of beauty and could never take it out of the box.

I couldn't resist. I carefully took the ring out and slipped it onto my left ring finger. I held it out and gasped. Every time I moved even the slightest bit it winked at me. There was a knock on my door and I gasped, dropping the box onto the floor. The velvet holder popped out of the bottom and it lay there in pieces.

"Oh, damnit!"

I dove for the box and tried to put it back together with shaking hands. What if it was Kent knocking on my door? He was going to see me being ridiculous. Or worse yet, he was going to think that I had accepted his proposal.

The knocking sounded again.

"Elly? Are you home?"

I froze. It was Stacy. Oh, thank God! I got up off the floor and opened the door, peeking my head out.

"Hey," I said, shoving my body in the doorway so she couldn't come in.

"Hey. Kent called me and said you might need someone to come babysit you. Everything alright?"

"Mhmm, yep. I'm good. You don't have to waste your time with me. I'm sure you've got more important things to do."

I watched her brow furrow as her all-seeing eyes did a quick examination. "Yeah, I think I have to come in."

"No!... Um, no, it's a mess," I insisted, trying to hide the panic in my voice.

She tried to push the door open but I held it firm. "Elly. Come on. Let me in. It's not fair that you're pregnant, I can't very well physically fight you. What are you hiding in there? A man?"

Oh, if only.

"No. I'm not hiding anything. Except the mess that is my apartment."

"Alright. Fine." She retreated, hands raised in defeat.

"I'll call you later." I was so relieved that she wasn't going to catch me in my lies that I didn't even think about it when I waved goodbye with my left hand.

The damn diamonds twinkled like a glittery poster and instantly caught her attention.

She ran towards me, squealing. "Elly! Oh my god!! Let me see that!" Before I could react she grabbed my hand and pulled it toward her face. "Oh, that's stunning."

I pulled my hand back and retreated into my apartment. My cover was already blown. The box was still scattered on the floor and the corner of it cut into the sensitive flesh of my foot. "Ow!" I hopped backwards.

"What in the world...?" Stacy asked, mystified as she entered my apartment and looked at the battered box on the floor.

I whimpered as I sat down on the floor and rubbed my foot. "I just wanted to try it on. And then you knocked and scared me. I'm going to put it back together right now." I sighed as I moved towards the mess and started putting it back together.

Stacy was still standing, watching me until I was finished.

"Success," she said with a grin. "Oh wait, what's this?" She leaned down and picked up a folded white slip of paper. She opened it and her eyes nearly bugged from her head. "Jesus." She held the paper out to me and I quickly looked it over.

Tiffany & Co.
Fifth Avenue and 57th Street
New York, NY 10022

Sales Professional: Jeremy

tore: 0100	Reg: 001	Trans: 1441/t
06/10/12	RSP: 12354	Take/1

PLAT PNK SOLESTE CUSH	18,100.00
PLAT INFIN BRAC	225.00
CHM ELE	125.00
CHM NOTE	125.00
CHM CPCK	125.00
SUBTOTAL	18,700.00
7.00%	1,309.00
TOTAL	20,009.00

I looked over it again. And then again. He had spent twenty grand? I glanced at my finger and then at my bare wrist. I glanced back at the receipt and felt my heart stutter. He bought this for me on the day of my birthday. Suddenly I felt sick to my stomach and had to sit down.

"Woah there." Stacy came beside me and put her hand on my back. "Sticker shock?"

"No, he...look at the date." I shoved the receipt into her hand. She took the receipt from me and snorted. "Well, I'll be damned. That would have been a sweet birthday present."

"He gave me the charm bracelet because Bryan had announced that we were dating at my party." I closed my eyes tightly and shook my head. This wasn't happening to me. I had chosen the wrong man, clearly. I had done what Kent had done so long ago to me. He'd picked the wrong girl and we'd both paid for it. And here I was trying to do the same thing and holding a grudge because I thought he didn't want me for me even though that was all he'd been saying for the past year. All he'd been doing the past year was trying to get me to see that he loved me, that he wanted to share his life with me.

I put a hand to my stomach and blew out a long breath. "I'm being such an idiot."

I glanced at Stacy, she was being awfully quiet.

She shrugged her shoulders, "Don't look at me. I agree. You're being an idiot. He clearly loves you even though it took him too long to admit that to himself. Maybe this baby was a blessing from God to try to push you two together."

I chuckled and gently tugged the ring from my finger. "Maybe." I gently placed it back into the box and then repackaged it. I worried my lip with my teeth as I stared at the box in my hands. "What if he changes his mind?"

Her hands squeezed my shoulders just before she stood up and offered up her hand. "Then he's a fucking idiot."

I took her hand she helped me up from the floor. "You're right."

She shrugged. "Yeah, that's not news to me." She embraced me and then stepped back with a grin. "Go get your man!" She blew me a kiss and then headed out the door, leaving me alone with an expensive engagement ring and memories of a torrid past.

"Go get my man... right..."

This was the scariest thing I'd probably ever have to do, and like a used band-aid, I was going to quickly rip it off and get it over with.

Chapter 37

Now or never, Elly. Now or never.

I blew out a hot breath as I approached Kent's front door. First I'd gone to his mom's house but he wasn't there. And now I was here, his SUV in the driveway confirmed that he should be home.

I teased my lower lip with my teeth as I reached for the doorbell. I had a flashback of college, of coming to him to confess my feelings only to see Jen standing in the doorway with his ring on her finger. I shook those away. It wasn't going to be like that this time. This time was going to be different.

I waited for a minute and then two. I glanced around his quiet neighborhood. Lights were on in pretty much every house. I looked back to Kent's door as it swung open. I held my breath, half expecting to see a naked woman standing there. But it was him. He had a towel around his hips, his hair still wet from the shower I'd obviously interrupted.

"Oh, God, I'm sorry. I'll come back later," I took one step back. His eyes flashed with fear and he grabbed my wrist and pulled me inside. He smelled like Irish Spring. My eyelids fluttered, trying not to get lost in it.

"Now is fine. Let me just get dressed, I'll be right back."

He took one step away before I grabbed onto his wrist. "Wait. Here." I tucked the box into his open palm and then took a step back. I couldn't tear my eyes away from his gorgeous face.

First it was puckered with confusion but slowly it transformed into shock, his mouth going slack. His eyes met mine and raised in question. "Is this a prank or something? Because I was serious about what I said."

I nodded. "I know. It's not a prank."

He was back to his confused state, his brows furrowing. "But I don't understand. What changed your mind? Just hours ago you said--"

I cut him off, "I know exactly what I said, Kent. I found something that proved that you were telling the truth."

"What did you find?" he asked, his voice filled with disbelief.

"A receipt."

"Ah, hell, Elly! You aren't supposed to know how much it cost. I have to take it back now." He turned away and stomped off towards his room with all the grace of a moody teenage boy.

"Kent!" I stayed where I was, though. I didn't dare follow after him in his current state of dress, or undress, as it happened to be. I sighed, my thighs clenching as I envisioned what he was doing back there. Did he want me to leave? Was he taking his proposal back now? I was about to sit down on his couch and wait when he stormed back out to the living room. He was dressed to go out. His hair mussed by the towel and his fingers. "Kent?" I asked as I watched him grab his wallet and his keys. "Do you want me to leave?"

"No. We're going to the jewelry store and they close in forty five minutes so we have to hurry."

It was my turn to frown. "What? We're not going to the jewelry store."

"Yes, we are. You know how much I paid for that ring."

"So?" I laughing because I had no idea how else to react. He was being crazy.

"So you weren't supposed to know," he insisted.

"Kent. You're being ridiculous."

"I'm not. Let's go," he commanded as he stepped towards his front door.

I followed him but with trepidation. I didn't want him to take the ring back. I loved it. We were silent as we drove. I wasn't paying attention as buildings passed by. My mind was stuck on Kent.

Were his feelings hurt? Had I hurt him? Was he changing his mind? Was this just an excuse to take the ring back and fall back on what he'd said to me? My mind was spinning when the car finally stopped.

I glanced around at our surroundings. We were not in front of a jewelry store. We were at Bella Noches. I was still staring when my car door opened and he reached in and grabbed my hand, helping me out.

"Come on, Elly. I've been waiting to do this for years."

My feet moved as he led me but my mind was still stuck in his car. Bella Noches. I hadn't thought about it for ages. My worst fears were realized here. My heart was pounding in my chest as I caught up with him, my mind firmly back in its rightful place.

"Dinner for two, please," he said to the hostess. As I stared on he reached for his wallet and pulled out some cash. He held it out to her and she nodded before turning away.

"Just a moment, please," she said.

Kent didn't look at me, his hand was still firmly holding mine, as if he didn't want to let me go. Or he didn't want me to run away from him. I had to admit I was tempted.

The hostess returned moments later and showed us to a private table near the back of the restaurant. It was set between the fireplace and a half wall that was topped with decorative glass. She set the menus down, murmured the server's name and then disappeared.

Kent pulled a chair out for me and took his place across from me after I'd sat down. The hard angles of his face showed in the dancing firelight.

"Are you alright?" he asked, a devilish grin on his lips.

All I could do was nod as I turned my attention back to my menu. The smart ass in me came out. "This is the weirdest jewelry store I've ever been to, by the way."

Kent chuckled as he set his menu down. I felt his eyes on me and after I'd settled on what I was going to eat I set my menu down as well. "So what is it going to be, Ms. Palmer?"

"I heard the chicken parmesan was to die for."

He smiled, his eyes dropped to the table for a moment before meeting mine. I felt myself melting in his gaze. "Those were not the words I used."

"I never said they were," I said as I grinned at him. "What are you going to have?"

"Oh, I'm not hungry. I'm just going to have a salad."

I kicked him playfully under the table at his teasing but he had done it. I was easing into this evening and whatever he'd had planned for it. When I glanced up he was smiling at me, something wistful in his eyes.

"So," I said, clearing my throat, "what are we doing here?"

"We're having dinner."

"Clearly. But why?"

He glanced at me, an accusing expression there. "Elly, can you just be patient?"

I scoffed and sat back in my seat. Something about that put a spur in my boot. Had he really just said that to me? Be patient? I'd been patient for decades!

"Yeah, sorry. I can't. I can't do this." All of my emotions came to a boiling head. All the years of being put on the back burner while he explored himself and Jen. And now he was finally ready. But was I? I hadn't even stopped to really think about whether or not I was really wanting to be married. He bought me a ring on my birthday and everything came crashing down. He had forced my hand and stirred up all of those emotions. He was telling me to jump and I was begging him to tell me how high.

I stood up from the table but his hand on my wrist stopped me from walking away.

"Elly. Where are you going?"

I met his confused eyes and shrugged my shoulders.

"I don't know but my patience has run out, Kent. Especially

where you are concerned."

He fell to his knees, grasping my hand in both of his. I glanced around the restaurant to see if people were staring. They were. How could they not stare at the desperate man who was grasping onto me?

"Elly, I'm sorry. That was crass and inappropriate. I just wanted this to be right. I didn't want to get down on my knees in my house. It took everything I had in me to keep it together until I could take us somewhere that meant something to us. I should have asked you in the eighth grade to go out with me. I should have asked you on your birthday when I'd taken you here. Or at least made out with you when we were alone together in my room right after. But I was a scared, dumb kid." He still held my hand tightly as he shifted, getting to one knee, his other hand pulled the ring box from his pocket. "I love you. I always have and I always will. Elly Marie Palmer..."

I held my breath as I stared back at him. No one else mattered at this moment. This was our moment. Finally. I felt the unwanted tears in my eyes. I didn't want to be one of those emotional women who couldn't control themselves but I couldn't help it.

Slowly he opened the ring box and presented it to me. "...will you marry me?" he asked. His hands were trembling and I saw the fear popping out on his brow in the form of moisture.

I sniffled as my mind raced to find the right thing to say. Here he was in front of me, finally. He was everything I'd ever wanted, flaws and all. We were together, we had the chance to be happy. Was I going to throw it all away because I was angry with him for taking so long to realize what I'd known for a long time? Rarely in life does a person get a third chance. But Kent was my best friend and the man I'd loved since I knew what the emotion meant. I would give him one hundred chances if that was what it took. I was stupid for him.

And suddenly the word came to me. "Yes."

It took him a moment to comprehend it but when he finally did he grinned and slipped the ring on my finger. It twinkled even brighter in the restaurant lighting. He got up to his feet and wrapped his arms around me. I closed my eyes and savored it. It had taken fifteen years but I was finally home.

BONUS

Sneak Peek into Fast Friends - Just Friends Series - Book 3

Oh my god, this guy is so hot.

It was all I could think about as his lips trailed down my neck, his hands deliciously palming my breast and my ass. He groaned when we fell backwards together on the cab's backseat as Christmas music played through its cheap speakers.

"Excuse me. This is not the appropriate place for that behavior. Stop or I will have to terminate your ride."

The words barely registered but the sudden loss of his body on top of mine had not. It was my turn to groan.

"Sorry," he whispered with his lust-laden voice, pushing a chunk of his long dark hair back behind his ear. I'd probably been the reason it had become dislodged from his ponytail in the first place.

He helped me to sit up straight and then threw his arm over my shoulder, hugging me in close to his side. I stared at the rearview mirror to make sure we weren't being watched and smiled sweetly as my hand found the outline of him through his dark jeans. I couldn't wait to feel it outside of its confined space.

He leaned over and nudged my temple with his nose. "You better quit or we'll be walking." He nipped my earlobe, sending tingles of delight through my body. He let out a low growl of pleasure as my hand moved to his thigh.

"Walking isn't the exercise I really had in mind," I murmured.

"Me either, Princess," he replied.

"Mmm." I snuggled against the powerful man who was cradling me, trying to center myself. I'd had too much to drink. Too, too much. I closed my eyes and let the car gently sway us. Vaguely I was aware that Jesus probably wouldn't approve of my getting sloshed on the day of his birth. But I considered this a present to myself since I hadn't received any other gifts this year.

The taxi lurched to a stop, causing me to gasp softly. Rio chuckled beside me. I looked up and caught a brief glimpse of his amazingly beautiful smile before he was ushering me out of the warm cab and onto the street. I stared at his ass as he reached back into the cab to pay for the ride.

So tight. I just wanted to—

"Hey!" He chuckled as he spun around and swatted at my fingers, which were pinching him.

I giggled as he grabbed both my hands and pulled me against his warm chest.

"Hey," I said, my voice sounded weirdly sexy to my own ears.

He stared at me for a moment, his panty-dropping expressive blue eyes searching mine for something. Before I could ask what he was looking for, his lips came down on mine. It was as if something had exploded in my body and for the hundredth time that evening I wasn't sure if I was going to be able to walk when his arms eventually left my backside. He pulled away and I whimpered at the loss. His chuckle was deep and harsh.

"Just up a few stairs. Then I promise I'll strip you down. Piece by piece."

His words sent shivers through my body. I bit my lip to keep myself together. The last thing I needed was my body in a puddle on the sidewalk in front of his house. I paid no attention to my surroundings, my eyes focused solely on his ass. Oh my god. His ass. I couldn't wait to dig my heels into it.

I stumbled up the concrete stairs and watched as he pulled some keys from somewhere. Maybe that's what the little poking had been in the cab. I registered a little pain as I bit the inside of my mouth.

Shit.

My hands curled into fists as he fumbled with the key in the lock.

Hurry up, hurry up!

Finally, he got the lock open and pushed the door open. He waited for me to go first, which I thought was super charming, and I went inside. I glanced around quickly noting that it was a bit messy. But it didn't smell bad and I didn't see any critters. I pulled off my shoes, holding onto a white wall as I did so, my back towards most of the house. He was so heavenly to look at that I was having second thoughts. Maybe he was realizing his mistake. Maybe he was thinking that he shouldn't be with some slutty girl he met at the bar. Maybe...

My thoughts were interrupted by his lips. The sound of his keys hitting the floor barely registered above his sexy ass moaning and the excitement of my back hitting the wall. He stole my breath, my gasp swallowed by his delicious lips. The scratchiness of his short beard mixed with the gentleness of his hands on my hips was driving me crazy. My hands went to his pants, I didn't want to waste any more time. My body curved towards his, his belt jingling between us.

His pants fell just enough to open and reveal his cock struggling against the inside of his black boxer briefs. His hands started to roam after he removed my coat and let it drop to the floor. It pooled behind my feet. His hands continued their exploration, moving towards my tits which were aching for his touch. I groaned and ground myself against him as I lifted my hands up, helping him to get my shirt off.

"I can't wait to feel how you feel inside me."

"Just a little longer," his gravelly voice answered me as he lifted the shirt free. He kissed me once more and pulled me towards his couch, stripping my clothes from me, as promised, along the way.

"That's enough talking," I said as I stripped off his leather jacket and then his shirt and tossed them haphazardly across the room. I fell back with him onto the couch, my lips seeking his again. His hands pushed everything down his hips before he let his body come towards mine.

I groaned in frustration. Too slow! I shifted and pushed him down onto the couch and climbed on top of him. I kissed him, my center pressed against him. I gasped as he filled me. It was slow, sweet torture. His hands on my hips held me in place as he claimed me.

* * *

I woke up with a sharp gasp and groaned as my hand touched my forehead which was pounding louder than the thumping of the bass in the bar last night. My eyes raked over the ridiculously hot man lying beside me and slowly the night started coming back to me.

Oh god, what had I done?

This had been a mistake. Did I really want to be with a guy who took a total stranger to bed? He probably did this kind of thing all the fucking time.

Shit!

I pushed my hair back from my face and quickly tumbled out of his bed. What was I doing? Oh my god, oh my god! Elly was totally going to know that I boned him.

And so what if I had boned him? No, that wasn't the right attitude. This was so bad. I had just confessed to her before her open mic how much I wanted a stable guy. A good guy. A guy that I could take home to my mother and say, 'See! This is what a fucking good guy looks like, Mom. They aren't that hard to find!' But this wasn't that guy. This guy was in a band. He had so many tattoos he drew the eye towards him, and he probably had lots of casual sex while high on drugs. I didn't need that kind of guy.

Shit!

I crawled out of bed and tip-toed to his bathroom. After I cleaned myself up and swallowed some Tylenol I found in his cupboard, I crept back out to gather my clothes. I paused beside the bed and stared at him one last time. He was still sleeping. My fingers itched to move some of his long, dark wavy hair from his cheek. There was nothing I wanted to do more than climb back into bed with him. But I couldn't do that. He was bad news and forbidden. Still, I couldn't help myself as I snapped a quick picture on my phone before zipping out to his living room. I pulled on all of my discarded clothes in a hurry and made it safely out of his house.

It wasn't until I was a few houses down that I realized I'd forgotten my bra. Ah, well, something for him to remember me by. Or something for him to add to his collection, if he had one. Whatever.

As I walked down the street and called the number for a cab, I couldn't help but wonder how many other girls he'd been with, and I struggled to remember if we'd used protection.

"Jesus, Stacy," I reprimanded myself openly as I smacked myself on the forehead. I could have any number of diseases. What the fuck had I been thinking? Right. I'd been thinking that he was fucking sexy and that I wanted to have his babies. How fucked up was I?

I walked a few more blocks before the cab pulled up. My mind was on Elly as I rode home. I hope I hadn't messed up her chance at being in a solid band. I wasn't sure if Rio would call her. Hell, I wasn't even sure his band was legit. It was probably just a line, his way to get me into his bed. He had certainly been successful. He was charming, for sure. Too bad I wasn't going to speak to him again until I was fully committed and/or married to the man of my dreams. The kind of man who never had a one night stand and would never even see the merit of having one.

I paid the cab driver, tip and all, and did my walk of shame to my apartment. It was a downstairs studio apartment with an external door all its own, and it was smaller than tiny, but it was mine. And I had paid for it all on my own.

I didn't want to think about that right now either. I had work in two hours. Back to the grindstone for me.

This is the end of your Fast Friends Preview. Don't forget to pick up the next in the series. Stacy and Rio's hot, sexy Happily Ever After is waiting for you.